The Spanish Painter

Devora Rogers

Copyright © 2017 Clavius Media, LLC

All rights reserved.

No portion of this book may be reproduced in any form without permission from the publisher, except as permitted by U.S. copyright law.

Cover design by Masha Beversdorf.

Title font credit: ADAM.CG PRO

First edition, 2017.

www.spanishpainterbook.com
ISBN: 1979472815
ISBN 13: 9781979472814

For Flores, who told me stories

When you have buried us told your story
ours does not end we stream
into the unfinished the unbegun
the possible . . .
to bring each other here
choosing ourselves each other and this life
whose every breath and grasp and further foothold
is somewhere still enacted and continuing

-Adrienne Rich, from *Dream of a Common Language*

The duende's arrival always means a radical change in forms. It brings to old planes unknown feelings of freshness, with the quality of something newly created, like a miracle.

-Federico García Lorca

Cuenca, Spain 1978

She prepared the room for the young woman's arrival. Every detail was in order. She counted them on her fingers to make sure. Three thick white towels she'd washed then let hang from the windows all night (she always said the moonlight brightened them) then ironed and folded tenderly, leaving them stacked neatly on a small wooden chair in the bathroom. Ten wooden hangers that smelled of cedar in the wooden cabinet she'd found and brought up from the street, then refinished herself. The large ceramic bowl filled with pears, apples, oranges and a handful of figs. One small plate with fresh pound cake—the secret was she used olive oil and yogurt—everyone else in Cuenca used vegetable oil for baking, but the olive oil was softer. By the time she'd sung to it and let it rise in her oven downstairs, then sprinkled it with powdered sugar, the taste that kept everyone from using olive oil had gone. She'd leave her a few slices each day till the girl got settled and knew where to buy her bread. She counted the items then quickly checked the small tiled bathroom with its tiny window looking out to the hills below. Yes, she'd remembered to leave a bar of her best French soap. The American girl probably wouldn't know the difference between homemade Spanish soap and this smooth little bar she'd bought from an herbalist in Paris. But the girl would feel how soft it left her skin and without knowing exactly how or from where, she'd feel comforted. Of this, Carmen was sure. Clean towels, hangers, fresh fruit, homemade *bizcocho*, French soap. What had she left out? Did American girls drink beer? Perhaps she'd leave her a few fresh *cervezas*—who wouldn't enjoy one after a long journey? She turned around slowly but with purpose. Yes, she'd left the windows open so the cool spring air would keep the apartment fresh. The rose geraniums were just ready to be set in the window sills, they wouldn't bloom till June, but they'd be pretty in the window and the girl could enjoy them throughout the summer. Carmen hoped she would like her. She didn't know what 21-year-old girls from New York liked to eat or do with their time.

Of course, whoever the girl was, it didn't matter whether Carmen liked her. This was a favor to Zorita. Federico Zorita, the most generous patron in Cuenca had asked her to look after the girl. Carmen owed Federico everything, and she'd never deny him. But even if Zorita had not asked her, she would give this girl what she gave all their guests: The cleanest, most peaceful, warm place they'd ever known. She'd wash her clothes, bed sheets and socks. Make the bed for her. Leave her soaps and *guisos*. Carmen didn't have to do any of this. But she was a caretaker by trade—it was her art in the same way canvas was his. And maybe, although Carmen knew she would care for the girl like any other who passed through their home, in a secret and small space, maybe she hoped the girl would be different. She was an intellectual, of course. She would not be interested in Carmen's homemaking arts or her homemade *salsas*. But maybe they would form a friendship. She'd always wanted a girl of her own.

Carmen did not dare speak it out loud. She'd be laughed at by the painters—an unfulfilled and too eager mother they'd say, let the girl be. *Déjala*, they'd say, she's here for art, not a mother.

After a final inspection, Carmen bent over, sweeping her hand across the freshly made bed, seeing to it there wasn't an uneven line between the sheets, then smoothed her apron and stepped out into the hall, locking the one room apartment behind her with quick strokes. She hoped the girl would be happy here.

Chapter I

When I was 16, I learned my mother had been lying to me all my life. It was a big and terrible lie, as lies between mothers and daughters often are. The lie of origin is the worst betrayal of all.

In some ways, you always knew, you always suspected you were not who you were told you were. You could feel it in your bones, even in your name. Something didn't sit right. The homesickness, the unbelonging. That was there, before I knew the truth. Before I pushed it out of my mother at 16, without even knowing what I'd done or how. Later, you look back and see all the signs pointing to that big flashing "lie!" You look into your own face, see your olive skin, black eyes and thick black eyebrows, and you almost laugh—of course! Of course you came from something else, someone else. Your blood, your root, never quite at home.

In the end, it was the bulls that gave it away. With the bulls, the truth came out, bloody and covered in goo, like an afterbirth of some half-human, half-alien being: Messy, painful, with a lot of explaining to do.

Before I knew anything, since I'd been little, I'd drawn on everything I could find. Every piece of paper, loose strand, napkin, I'd scribble on. My mother hated this habit and she expressed her distaste frequently, mostly when we were in public and I'd disappear at the restaurant table into my pen and napkin doodle. Or that is what she called it. "Stop doodling, Izzy!" I heard that refrain more often than any expression of love. My mother had raised me and loved me, but without gusto—or any that could be seen and measured. She always seemed closed up and tight, like a flower that forgot to bloom. Or maybe once she had bloomed, but she'd never tell of it now. On the few occasions when she embraced me, her arms always felt stiff and brittle. There'd never been a home in her.

By my teenage years, the "doodling" had turned into an obsession. After dinner, dishes and homework, I'd hole up in my room with the work lights blazing, Iggy Pop blasting, and oils oozing out of their tubes onto increasingly life-sized canvas. *So messed up I want you here…In my room I want you here…And now I want to be your dog…Now I want to be your dog.*

I didn't know what I was painting or how. Only that the one thing I wanted to be in the world was a painter. Despite the fact my mother was a curator at LACMA, she was nonplussed to have a painter on her hands—having an *abstract* painter for a daughter was intolerable to her. Like the chef who refuses to cook for his family, she had no patience for painters. The lights, in particular, she hated for their "exaggerated effect" as she often called it. "Is that really necessary, Izzy?"

I didn't care. It was the only thing that got me through high school and life under my mother's roof. During my teenage years we drew wide circles around each other, our conversation often punctuated by nasty remarks with a substance and tone so cruel that only a mother and daughter could master it.

The question of my father had long ago been settled, leaving me with little alternative to my mother's company. The story went like this: Finance executive/from Manhattan/just together for a short time (she started using the words "one night stand" by the time I was in my early teens) /lost touch/got back in touch/then he died of an early heart attack/no family remaining. When I was younger, I would ask about him occasionally, mostly to my mother's extreme and total annoyance.

"But you don't have any photos at all?"

"Izzy, it was just an affair. I didn't take any photos. It wasn't like today where everyone has a disposable camera everywhere they go."

"How did you meet him? What was he like?"

"What does it solve, Izzy? He was effectively a sperm donor."

My mother was a tight-lipped bitch when she wanted to be. I never got anywhere with those conversations. So I grew up telling people, "I don't have a dad." What else was I to say? There was no evidence to the contrary, and whoever he was, he was clearly not interested in me.

Instead of a father, I had my painting. I had set up a larger than life-sized canvas in my room. I would cover the floor in old drop cloths I'd procured from a neighbor and listen to Leonard Cohen on repeat for hours. My mother came and went while I holed up there, content with my solitude, unhappy with everything else.

It started with strange little birds with their little claws and wings and beaks. They were simple creatures and asked nothing of anyone. Then the bulls came. I began dreaming of a brave *torero* gone awry. Each dream was the same: A handsome, young matador begins his bull fight with spectacular courage, full of naive, but beautiful bravado. His moves are flawless, the audience sits in silence, captivated. But then, when it is time to turn from artistry to the killing, he is unable to slay the beast swiftly—the one sacred vow a matador makes to the bull. After stabbing the bull repeatedly with his spear, he leaves the ring, shamed, covered in blood, the bull left to die in the ring, the crowd booing and shouting in anger. I would awaken terrified, yet longing for the bright colors and melodic reverie to be my life and not just a nightmare waking me from my lonely teenage existence.

The bulls never left me after that first dream. The minute I awoke, I set paint to canvas. Without knowing from where, there were feet and massive bodies and sharp horns. I did not paint true to life, these were abstract creatures—made of blues and yellows, pinks and greens. They were angry and they were hungry. And also fearless. I loved them.

The bulls stayed with me for months.

You know when you're painting bulls with fangs on canvas at 16 that something is not entirely right. And you suspect by the time your cognitive mind has formed that it didn't come from a "finance guy" from Manhattan. This narrative would have continued without disruption had it not been for the bulls.

I'd been working on one bull for weeks. This one was raw—I had let him go completely to the dark side. There were women in distress around him, their bodies exposed, his horns piercing their insides. It was a terrible scene. But there he was across my canvas, defiant.

I was stuck on what to do with the background—I always struggled with the white space—how much emptiness to leave, how much *not* to paint. He was nearly finished, but I was worried about stifling him with too much "interference" as an art teacher of mine liked to call it. So I left him there for the night, hanging from the wall. He seemed to own the room, while also appearing to be a victim to it. If my mother could have been an objective observer, even she would have agreed it was good work. *Nice, Izzy. Pretty good,* I told myself as I switched off the work lights and headed out to see friends. "Hanging out" with friends typically involved hot-boxing ourselves in someone's car in front of someone's parents' house and then spending the rest of the evening huddled in a booth at Denny's. The truth was I liked painting better than this excuse for a social life, but these nights were the best I could do to get out of my mother's house and not feel completely isolated from the world.

Hours later, still slightly buzzed from cheap weed, I let myself back into our dark house, tiptoeing through the hall to my bedroom, certain my mother was asleep by now. She went to bed and rose early, something that enabled us to see as little of each other as possible. Being near each other was awkward, we had nothing to say to one another and for years it had felt as though we genuinely didn't like one another. I sincerely doubted things would ever change between us. While I didn't know it then, what happened that night was the start to closing the deep divide between us.

I returned to my room stoned and ready to paint. I was looking forward to connecting with my bull. I never expected to find my mother there instead. Oddly, when I found her, she appeared to have taken on his traits. There she was, cross-legged on her haunches, the universe around her in tatters, her head thrown back in anger, her hands wringing in her lap, her blondish grey hair matted across her forehead, and above all this—tears streaming down her face. A simple fact occurred to me then: I'd never seen my mother cry.

The words that went through my mind were, *This is not my mother.* The only answer that my logical mind could provide was that this woman before me was simply *not my mother.* And in a way, she *wasn't.* Later, looking back I realized I wasn't entirely wrong. The mother I'd known for sixteen years was a lie. This mother—the soft cheeked, salt-eyed woman on the floor—was someone entirely different. She appeared more vulnerable than she'd ever let me see her before.

My mind tried to put the pieces together to make sense of what was happening. As I saw her there on the floor, looking both much older and younger than I'd ever seen her, suddenly I understood. I just *knew.* How do you know something like that? How does your gut know? The real question is how you could *not* know. And I knew. With every piece of me, I knew what had brought my mother to her knees.

The bulls had called my mother's bluff.

My mother looked up at me as I stood in the doorway of my room, bewildered; her green eyes were wide, and her cheeks, tear-stained.

"Your father is a painter." Then almost inaudibly, she said, in perfect Spanish, "*Un pintor español.*"

I looked at her, mute, incapable of speaking. We stared at each other for several minutes till she broke the silence.

"That's what you wanted isn't it? To know?"

I remained motionless, frozen with this unanticipated revelation.

"Well, Izzy," my mother said through sobs, "Isn't that what you wanted?"

I peeled my lips apart nearly forcibly to respond. There are those moments so tense, so full of emotion that pausing the entire world for about 48 hours and saying nothing seems like the only answer.

But no, here she was, finally opening up to me about something I'd long known in my heart I didn't have the full story about. I had to keep her talking.

"Shit, Mom. Why did you lie about some finance guy? Why did you bother? Why did you wait so long to tell me?"

My mother looked at me with horror as I responded to her with question after question. I watched as her face changed and it dawned on her what her emotional outburst had unleashed. I realized I had to act fast if I wanted to catch her before she closed up again.

"Can I call him?"

My mother was recovering from her vulnerable position. She stood up, wiping her eyes.

"Izzy, what do you mean, *call him*?"

"You know, call him. On the telephone. Introduce myself. Say hello."

My mother sighed with a deep irritation. I could see her reaching for a reason that would satisfy me, anything to keep me from asking more about my father.

"Izzy, we've been through this."

"No, Mom, we haven't been through this. This just started tonight, when I found you in my room sobbing on the floor in front of a painting of a fucking bull. We haven't been through anything."

"That's all there is to tell."

"That he's a Spanish painter? That's your idea of 'all there is'?"

"What makes you think he wants to hear from you anyway?"

"I don't know, I'm his daughter, he's my father. Maybe he'd like to hear from me. What's his name?"

"You're young Izzy—"

"Tell me his name."

"—You think everything is possible.

"What's his name?"

"Izzy. Sometimes things aren't possible. Sometimes things don't work out."

I had never really considered that the man I'd started to think of as my father might not *want* to know me. I feigned confidence:

"What's the worst that could happen?" I asked.

I watched my mother eye the doorway as if looking for an escape route. She appeared genuinely panicked. I looked at her, realizing she was holding on to the information, *my story, my origin* as if it were something to own, as if it belonged to her. I knew better. This was *my* story.

As we stood there, our bodies, mother and daughter, turning to stone, I caught a glimpse of myself in the mirror across from my bed. My wavy, chestnut brown hair fell around my face, cropped just below my ears. My eyes were big and round and brown—not green like my mother's—but terribly and profoundly brown. It occurred to me that maybe this man whose identity my mother had finally begun to reveal, whose face I'd never seen, might have given me these eyes, this nose, even my long neck—none of which resembled my mother. I imagined calling him; I could hear the conversation, *our* conversation—his voice scratchy and deep, covered with years of tobacco. I would use my high school Spanish, we could talk, we could meet. I heard the dial tones, the sound of the receiver picking up.

—¿Diga?

—Hola, soy Izzy, hija de Rebecca.

—¿Quien es?

—Hello, uh, hi, this is, Izzy, Rebecca Stern's daughter. I'm calling for my father. Do you know who I am?

—Claro que te conozco. *Of course.*

My heart leapt—he knew me! He expected my call, he was waiting to hear from me! I exhaled, relieved as my mind raced. I could not wait to ask him more—to talk with him, meet him, maybe go to Spain—

—Isabel—

He said my name in a way I had never heard anyone say it before. He said my name as if he had always spoken it. Eeh-sah-belle. Eeh-sah-belle. No one had ever called me by that name, not like that.

Eeh-sah-belle.

In those three syllables I felt something I'd been looking for my entire life. Not Izzy. Not Ih-zah-bel. But Eeh-sah-belle.

—Isabel—I heard my name again. I looked up to see not an aging Spanish painter with a hand rolled cigarette in his hand but my thin, graying, perma-frost mother.

"Izzy, there is no future with him. I'm sorry."

I breathed in deeply and my eyes turned back to my mother. Teenagers don't often examine their parents. They look at them, they project onto them, but they don't observe, see their lines and soft edges. They don't know yet what it means to watch life do things to you, change you, till you resemble nothing of who you were. But at that moment, I examined her as I never had before. She had stood up, and was looking at me softly. For a moment, I almost forgave her. *Look at her there*, I told myself; *she's soft, and sweet. Go to her, hold her hand.* And if I were to relive this moment again, maybe that's what I would have done. I would have sat down and asked her things; I would have wrapped my arms around her and cried with her. I would have remembered she was human and even if it came years too late, at least she'd let me in. But I was sixteen and I hated her. She would not let me have the one thing I'd always wanted: To know my father—to know my story.

I felt the anger surge, overcoming all thoughts of reconciliation. I felt the bitterness that she'd led me on for so many years. Most of all, I was furious that the place in me that never felt at home had been right—and she'd tried to convince me otherwise. I thought for a moment what I could say that would hurt her the most. What I could say that would, like a punch in the face, hit her back with the lies she'd sold me. Two words came:

"Get out."

I left her standing in the middle of my room and turned off the light and crawled in bed. My mother remained frozen where I'd left her. "Get the fuck out!" I growled again from beneath my covers. My heart was racing but the shock of my mother's revelation shut down my body like the light switch I'd turned off. The door slammed shut and I fell back into my bed, spent. I slept immediately. That night the bulls came to me in my sleep again. This time, I was in a bullfighting ring, behind a barrier near where a terrifying bull was released. I watched in horror as the bull entered the ring, wild-like, then turned and looked me right in the eye, then headed straight for me, ramming repeatedly into the barrier I stood behind. With each pound of his massive body, the barrier seemed to come loose and the bull would not stop. I awoke covered in sweat, just as the barrier broke in half and the bull's horns aimed at my jugular. My breath was quick and my pulse racing as I pulled myself out of the nightmare. And then I remembered what had occurred and suddenly, I felt lighter than I had ever felt. *I was right.* All along I'd been right. I wasn't from nowhere and nothing. The bulls helped me dig up a wild root my mother had tried to bury. The secret broke open and swam around inside me.

Wherever he was, whoever he was, I would find him.

Chapter 2

My mother's late night, bull-induced confession opened many more questions than it answered. Aside from the questions I had about my father, and the origins of my birth, who was this woman I used to know as my mother? My mother was a small, 95-lb middle-aged news junky who wore glasses, liked Indian take-out and lived her life through her work in art. She did not take well to animals or children. She did not spend time abroad. She did not create art, she catalogued it. She sneered at artists such as De Kooning and called them masochistic. My work she called 'unfocused.' Who was this person inside my mother who had lived, however briefly with a man—a painter, a *Spanish painter*—whose name I'd never heard her speak of once in my life?

When I woke in the morning, I tucked questions about my mother into a dark corner. I was furious at her intransigence but grateful for one thing. Her revelation had given me a gift—the knowledge that I'd been right. I knew. I'd *always* known. Now, I had a story. The bulls, the painting, the sense of not belonging—it wasn't from nowhere and nothing.

So I began to imagine him. Of course I put everything into creating an image of him in my mind. In my mind he was everything my mother could not be: Funny and charming, smooth and cool, temperamental and passionate all at once. In my imagination he was a talented, tortured painter. He stayed up nights painting and paid no attention to his health. He spoke with his hands and deep-throated gestures. He knew my name, but devotion to his art kept him preoccupied. Nonetheless, he too looked sometimes to the doorway for my arrival. Almost willed me there.

Spanish painter. I said the words over in my mind endlessly in English and Spanish. *Pintor. Español.* Spanish. Painter. *Pintor español.* I was like a teenage girl in love, writing her name in cursive with her boyfriend's last name appended to hers to see how it looks. *Pintor español.* Spanish painter. It was enough to keep my 16-year-old mind occupied for months. I came back often to my mother's assertion "there is no future with him" (which felt like an accusation) and wondered if we really had no future together.

We did not speak of him or our conversation again. It seemed so massive, so awful that neither of us dared to touch it. What was the point if she would not help me find him? But I was resolved: However long it took, I would learn where I came from and who my father was.

I finished high school. My prerequisite for college was that it had to be more than 3,000 miles or four hours by plane, train or car from my mother. I needed space from her. Several states seemed like a good distance, and I think my anger covered all of them with gobs of thick, hardened oil paint. I also needed more room to imagine this man, was who was partly responsible for my life. I signed up for courses on American identity, the history of consciousness and the impact of jazz on Western music. And of course, Spanish.

My college roommate and I didn't connect but we didn't clash. We agreed on just enough music and just enough politics to tolerate sharing a room, but we didn't let each other into our private worlds. In fact, I didn't really find anyone to let into my private world—not my roommate, not friends, not a boyfriend or girlfriend (I would have been open to one or the other). I was still burrowed too deep inside myself to be vulnerable to anyone. Anyway, there was only one person I wanted to know—everyone else seemed like window dressing.

Without telling anyone, I began to look for him. For $6.00, I'd secured a weekly source of Spanish news content via the *El País* Sunday paper from the local coffee house and book shop. The Spanish daily was five days old by the time it got to my little college town in Ohio; I got it a day after that. But I didn't care—I would go back to my dorm room with the paper under my arm like a secret government file. I read it obsessively—back to front, up and down. I circled words I hadn't learned in AP Spanish. I marveled at the color printings of art pieces appearing in new exhibits. I clipped my favorite articles and saved them. I made secret collages with the Spanish headlines like coded messages.

In every article I read, every photo I clipped, he was there. Or I wanted him to be, and so I found traces of him there.

The stories I clipped were about lots of things: About bullfighters like José Tomás, the bravest, most stylish *torero* who the critics called "modern"; the explosion of 300 meteorites in the last eight years; the rescue of people found in over-packed smuggling ships in the Gulf of Aden. In November, just as I was studying for finals, the biggest oil spill Spain had ever seen took place off the coast of

Galicia. Black oil spots covered the rocks and killed off oysters, shellfish and the livelihoods of fishermen. The paper showed pictures of the desperate captain of the sunken ship, and of groups of fishermen who went out in meager boats to clean, one splotch of oil at a time, though their efforts were hopeless against the oily plague. For weeks the newspapers reported on the disaster. Always there was an emotional fisherman who cried for his stricken sea and the years it would take for the oysters to ever be the same. As I read, tears would well up in my throat, as if it had been my sea, as if I had known her and loved her as they had.

Those nights tearing apart Spanish papers in my room filled me with hope. Somewhere, somebody shared my blood and my root. I didn't ask if he wanted to see me, I simply began to live in a world where he existed.

Chapter 3

FOUR YEARS I held those words in my hands. "Your father is a painter. A Spanish painter." *Pintor. Español. Pintor español.* I often whispered these words as I drifted off to sleep like a prayer or mantra.

And then—a year before the new millennium—in 1999, when I was 20, I had my first and best chance to get closer to uncovering the truth about my father. My painting had earned me a scholarship to study fine art for a semester in France. I accepted the department's offer without hesitation, though I didn't care about France. I wanted Spain. I wanted to find my father. As I packed my things in my university apartment, I looked through my journals. They were heavy with Spain. Sticky and fat pages that stuck to each other, living among my books and pencils like hidden cats or stowaway children. Glued images of writers, politicians, domestic abuse cases, human interest profiles. I would let them guide me to him. I could hear them breathing at night, breathing through their paper mouths, their spines heavy with my longing, my one wish: To know him.

Although she would not say so, a semester abroad wasn't something my mother wanted for me—just like the bulls, the work lights, and the paintings of my teen years. I could see her weighing if she could forbid me to travel across the border to Spain. That she said nothing convinced me she knew it would drive me faster in the other direction.

My mother knew there was a place she could not tap, a place that was not open to her. This place held my journals of Spanish newspaper clippings. It held the lie of origin she'd made for me. It held the man who refused to own me, or never had been asked to. I didn't know how it had happened, or who my mother was then for me to have been fathered by a painter in Spain. I knew only that the story she'd passed off for most of my life was not true. I didn't know what she was hiding, but I would be on the first train to Spain to find out.

My school was located in the South of France, in Toulouse where Lautrec had painted French prostitutes with chalk and abandon. I spent my first five days there hiding in the Gothic former abbey that housed several Lautrec paintings along with some of Southern France's most prized art collections: *Musée des Augustins.* I sulked in the inner courtyard, between the balustrades, sketching the stone cats with their mouths agape. "What stories you could tell," I whispered to them. The fifth day I spent staring at one painting in particular, Edouard Debat-Ponsan, Le Massage. *Scène de Hammam*, 1883. Surrounded by marble and intricate blue tile, a white woman lies stretched out on a marble slab, abandoned to the hands of her black-skinned masseuse. The light of the scene illuminates the white woman's body with near perfection. I watched this painting from opening till closing on a wooden bench in the upper museum.

On the sixth day I registered for classes I would not attend, paid the roommate the school had assigned me at the *Université Cité* to take care of my things, and I was gone. I told my mother nothing.

I left France seven days after arriving and forgot her immediately. On the train I watched the progression of train stations and sunset. The stations were painted in bright graffiti with missives like *"Mort aux fascistes."* France was beautiful but no matter how many tall church steeples called out or how many wild fields of yellow rape spread themselves across the train's path, I could not stay. What is France to the wilderness of Spain? What are her cathedrals and ordinary bells to this place where my father might still sit on a wooden crate with a beer and a cigarette to escape the heat in a cool, narrow alleyway? What is France to this place that lies only a strait away from Africa, once ruled by the Moors and their mighty swords?

"There is no future with him."

And still.

I've come.

Chapter 4

I BEGAN MY search. My French roommate advised me to rent a room with a Moroccan hostel owner named Omar she'd stayed with on previous trips to Spain. I had no idea where else to go. I took her advice and made my way by foot from a remote bus stop to a three-story hostel on the outskirts of the capital city. I arrived, sweaty and exhausted to *El Hostal Americano.* There were no Americans in sight and it looked little like anything I'd ever seen in America. But it was 2000 *pesetas* a night—the equivalent of 12 dollars—I would not find cheaper and I would be safe here.

I rang the buzzer and was let in by the graying but handsome Moroccan Daphne had referred me to.

As he opened the door he offered the polite but perfunctory "*Buenos días*" of someone who has welcomed thousands of strangers knowing he'll never see them again.

He pointed at the shared living spaces and walked me up the two flights of stairs to show me to my room. It was bigger than I'd expected, with a metal-framed bed and wooden table beneath the shuttered windows. I set down my bag and he pointed down the hall to a communal bathroom. In French-accented but perfect English, he recommended I try it out.

"The tub is good. It will refresh you after the afternoon heat and your journey. Very clean. Call me if you need anything." He turned to head down the stairs and left me in the darkened hall of the "American Hostel." If there were other guests there, I never saw them. I returned to my room and decided I would take up his tub recommendation.

It's the small things that break you apart. That's how it was with that green tub of Omar's. It wasn't the hash I'd smoke there. It wasn't the warmth of Omar's arms that would hold me when the tub could not. But that tub, *Christ* that tub. With its green tiles, its green porcelain basin—the shutters pulled tight to keep light and heat out during the hot summer Spanish days.

Pintor. Español. Everything was leading me to him. Once I'd gone to Spain, I knew I could not leave till I'd found my father. I dove into the journey head-first—the defiance to my mother had gotten me this far. But now that I was here, closer than I'd ever been to my father's home, I felt full of doubt and fear. I had never allowed myself to admit that embarking on this journey could break me apart. The grief of what I'd missed growing up with no father, with no idea of my origins—hit me hard.

As I sat in the bathtub, I looked around at the strange new surroundings I found myself in. And suddenly, I realized I didn't even know my own name. My skin unfolded and I watched my grief slam my bones into the green porcelain. My body was perfectly still beneath the surface of the water. But my bones were breaking. I realized I belonged to nobody and nothing and I would know nothing of myself until I found him. My tears flowed into that tepid water—how many tears I would cry in his tub. Omar and Spain, they pulled it out of me. What I'd been yearning for, dumb and silent to for 20 years. I emptied myself into Omar's tub.

He let me cry for an hour, then knocked gently at the door. When I answered with more muffled sobs, he turned the knob softly and entered the bathroom. He patted my head then handed me a towel.

"*Ven.* Whatever it is, you cannot solve it by crying all night. If it has a remedy then there is no need to cry. And if it has no remedy, there is no need to cry."

I stood up, strangely not shy to be tear-stained and naked in the presence of a man I'd met only an hour before. "Does this happen often? Girls coming here and crying in your tub? You appear to know what you're doing."

He shook his head with a click of his tongue and nodded at the candy bar wrapper and brown cube peeking out of tinfoil on the counter. I had picked the cube up from a gypsy outside the train station. She had brown, leathery skin and offered either rosemary sprigs or hash. I had assumed a gypsy selling rosemary couldn't be half bad and paid her a wad of *pesetas* for a fistful of hash wrapped in aluminum.

Omar shook his head, "You can't live on hash and Snickers bars. *Même sur les vacances.*"

Omar was right, my stomach turned that night. The high the gypsy had sold me was cruel. I spent two days curled in a ball on Omar's green and white checked floor, surrounded by walls with bright pink paint peeling at the corners. The walls closed in, their pink cells tightening around me. I watched beetles saunter by. I was too sick to care. I ate nothing and wretched for 40 hours. The world spun around me; showing me all of its ugliness and tragedy. I saw my fear, my anger, and my body heaved from the pain.

At the end of it, Omar tucked me into a large bed with a cool cloth over my head. I slept for nearly 18 hours. When I awoke, the sickness, the high, and the fever that started after my tearful bath had passed. But I was shaken. In my grief, I took to Omar's bed.

Being loved by him was unlike any other lover. He was no boy. He was tall, his arms fleshy, his belly rounding. He did not hesitate, he did not pretend or play games. He wanted me, and when he knew for sure I wanted him, he took me into his arms, salty and brown, and we made love.

We would talk after like old friends, not like two people who had just met when one of them fell apart in the other's community bathtub. There was 30 years of age between us, but it did not matter. Omar was like a companion I'd always dreamt of having. He did not judge me, he listened in ways guys my age could not, and we shared an easy, comfortable rapport. I had landed in Spain and fallen into the hands of the best friend I'd ever had. When Omar saw he could have the company of a young woman, he hung a "*Cerrado por descanso del personal*" sign on the door and we retreated to the interior of Omar's hostel, trading between the kitchen and his bedroom for four days. As Omar plied me with saffron rice and red wine, he told me stories of his home country and Spain. When he sensed I had relaxed, he began to pull me up from the earth, dusting off my sad edges as he went, a tender gardener pulling fruit from the soil.

"Is France not beautiful?"

I hesitated, unable to speak for fear the tears would start again. Omar watched me intently, caressing my hand with one hand as he sautéed the onions with the other. His presence was gentle and loving. I took a deep breath and tears began streaming down my cheeks.

"What do you run from, Isabel? Why have you come here now?"

"Omar, I didn't come for France. I've come to find someone."

"Someone? Do you have a lover here?"

"No. No lover. Except for you," I laughed, wiping my eyes.

"Who then?"

"I've come to find my father…"

It was the first time I had ever told another soul about my father.

Omar listened intently, letting me open to him.

"*Mi padre es pintor. Pintor español.*" I said the Spanish words that had run through my head years earlier, by the lamplight shining on a large bull on canvas. Omar stopped stirring the pan and looked at me intently.

"A painter?"

"Yes. I don't know much about him, though. He belonged to a group of painters who lived in Cuenca. Part of a group called *El Grupo* or something like that."

Omar's dark eyes stared at me with a furrowed brow. He appeared to look me up and down as if deciding if I was for real.

"What, what is it?" I asked him, impatient to understand his reaction.

"*El Grupo.* You're sure?"

"Yes, I'm sure, it's about the only thing I know, but I know that for sure."

"Fucking *El Grupo*?!" Omar shouted, then sighed with an *"Ai ai ai."* Omar shook his head. "Isabel, here I thought you were just another American. And you say one of the *El Grupo* painters is your father?"

"How do you—Do you know them?"

"*Claro.* Everyone knows them. This group is very well known in Spain. Molina, Torres. Regalado. Soto, of course. Do you know his name?"

"No, she refused to give me that. I went through her files one time and found an article about a collective named *El Grupo* in Cuenca, so I figured that would be a good place to start."

"*Su puta madre.* And you end up here in my shithole of a hostel. What are the chances?"

"Omar, if you know of them, maybe you can help me find him." Omar appeared to be examining me as if sizing me up anew; I could see he wanted to help.

"*Pues,* if one of these guys is your father, I know a man who ran with that group...I can't say for sure if he still knows where to find them all…but it's a start, no? If you find one of them, you'll get to the right one."

I looked at Omar with a mixture of awe and disbelief. To have landed at this forsaken place and fallen into his arms…two degrees from my father. The thought made me shiver.

As we sat by candlelight in the rundown hostel kitchen, I told Omar how I'd learned about my father, about my mother's lies and the defiant bull that kicked them out of her. I told him of my sticky Spain journals, the longing I had for this man who'd given me life. Omar listened with great care to my story. As we devoured the meal he'd made for us, I told him my greatest fear.

"What if my mother is right and once I find him, he doesn't want to see me?"

Omar didn't hesitate: "Do not listen to that fear. You have come this far. Do not stop until you learn who he is and where you come from. You must find him."

Omar said my name as I'd once heard it while imagining a conversation with my father. *Ee-sah-belle. Ee-sah-belle.* I looked up to see Omar looking at me intently and without doubt or fear. He was unafraid. And his loving helped *me* to be unafraid. With such faith in my journey, when he told me I had to continue on, I felt confident as I packed my things later that night. In the morning, I would continue my search for the Spanish painter who was my root.

Chapter 5

I TOOK A bus from Madrid to Cuenca. The train ride was long and unreliable so Omar advised me to go by bus. It was a long, hot journey that left me nauseous and parched. Only 100 miles separated Madrid and Cuenca but the journey took two and a half hours. There wasn't an *autobús directo* that morning so I took the local. The bus was like an old tortoise, slowly making its way around curvy hillsides, stopping every 15 minutes at rural bus shelters. I couldn't imagine how the old ladies supported by canes and orthopedic shoes got to the bus stops as they seemed to be in the middle of nowhere. But there they were, waiting by the side of the road. And we picked up every single one of them.

By the time we pulled into Cuenca, I'd have given my right arm to get off that bus. It was early afternoon and the sun was blazing down on me and my heavy backpack. I had literally no plan except to find the old guy Omar said might know something. I asked around for the bar Omar instructed me to head to. An old lady pointed up a steep hill where a sign pointed to the *Casco Antiguo.*

So I made my way up the hill. As the elevation increased, the road narrowed and the modern apartments of the new city below gave way to colorful old buildings with tiny wooden entryways.

Old, aproned women stood guard in front of their doors, alternating between polishing their brass door handles, yelling greetings, and admonishing passersby. I followed the main road, *Calle Alfonso VIII* towards the *Plaza Mayor.* There was not even an inch between each building; the only way you could tell it was a different building was that one would be red, another yellow, another bright blue, or deep grey. Later I learned that even the colors of the buildings didn't divide them neatly—the apartments stretched from one building to the next at random. One apartment could share a fourth story with one building, and a third story with another. Planters with rose geraniums hung from the windows, and clotheslines were strung up. It was now late afternoon and the town appeared to still be taking its *siesta.* Nothing is quite like a Spanish city during the *siesta*; it gave me a bit of quiet to take in the new scene, very different from the one I'd just experienced in Madrid. I walked through the *plaza*, past the tourist shops, past the cathedral, and up and down the uneven cobblestone streets of the old town. I peeked down stone-pocked lanes, wandered in and out of doorways belonging to *posadas* and tapas bars, and beneath the archways of former abbeys. Despite the fact I had no place to stay that night, and no understanding of how I would find my father, I was insatiable. After wandering for an hour or more, I made my way down a narrow pathway and came to a quiet stony terrace with a little church at one end. *Plaza de la Concepción*, read a small marker. With nothing but moss-covered stone and poplar trees, it looked like a scene out of a storybook. I turned to look behind me and saw Cuenca's old town hanging over the little church terrace, as if perched on the edge of a big rock. It was dusk, and the hillside was lit with the pink glow of the sun.

I knew then that I had come to the right place. With all my heart, I knew this city held secrets about my father and my birth. As I took in the cliffs of Cuenca, I was reminded of Jerusalem. My grandfather had taken me to the holy city for my Bat Mitzvah when I was 12. I was hundreds of miles from Jerusalem, but I felt the mystery of that place again here: Her Mediterranean shrubs of thyme, rosemary and lavender that grow from Athens to Safed; the length of the day and the lateness that falls the night; the soil that goes to sleep red and wakes up a crumbling limestone white; the fortressed city there in the distance, glowing like some cruel queen's pink gem. The old town perched above me, I could almost see him here, inside her walls somewhere.

People go to Jerusalem to find things, God or peace, or to follow a dream they believe was promised them there. The city vibrates with their hope. *Tu padre es pintor. Español. Pintor. Español.* I wonder if this city knows I have come with the same longing pilgrims bring to Jerusalem streets. I wonder if this city knows I am looking for some Western Wall to tuck a note into, with one wish—to know him.

I look again and perhaps the light has changed, but then I see, she isn't at all like Jerusalem, this town called Cuenca. And it isn't the Mount of Olives but a modest hill with a line of cell phone towers at the top. And I'm not at all sure now that she'll welcome me, I'm not sure she'll hear my longing and let her walls vibrate with the hum of my heart.

The light of dusk changes and once more, I see the city above, again anew. She is neither with me nor against me at all. She is simply there; her hanging houses in their cuts of hillside rock, the river gorges below and stone steeples above. Her walls and walls of stone. She does not know me, but yet, she does not refuse me. *She knew him.* I can almost smell him walking through her streets, *cerveza* and *cigarrillos* on his breath. Oil paint and remover on his hands, stained brown from tobacco and sepia ink. And perhaps from some window above, he sees me here on the hill, a wild, lonely beast come home to find her father.

I would tell him in broken Spanish:

> *I have dreamt of you for so long. It seems impossible to be here, impossible to find you, impossible not to try. Even if you refuse me, even if you tell me it is impossible and holler "Imposter!" Even if you are my father and I am your daughter, I know I have no claim to you—and my mother warned me long ago that we would have no future together. But my life is incomplete without you, my world is broken without this story, telling me where mine should begin. My life cannot go on without having tried to reach you, without having heard you speak my name, without having witnessed your home. For years I have imagined you—built you up, torn you down, painted your wild birds, your beastly* toros, *written your name, searched for you. I have learned your language in secret, studied your maps and come like a refugee across an ocean to find you.*
>
> *Will you admit me, will you say my name again, will you call me* hija *and tell me how this story came to pass?*

When I look to Cuenca's walls, they seem to say, it's been time enough, *ven aquí, tu padre está listo.* Come here, your father is ready.

Chapter 6

"El Grupo, ¿eh? ¿Qué tiene una chica americana que ver con unos hijos de puta como estos?" What has an American girl got to do with a bunch of sons of bitches like them?

Omar's "friend" was not quite what I had expected. He was an old man, with a big belly and scratchy voice that sounded mean. I couldn't tell if he was making fun of me or trying to help. Or maybe he was just enjoying himself. But either way, he was not exactly a sensitive human being.

José Luis ran a dark bar at the end of the *plaza* in the old town of Cuenca. Omar had told me that thirty years before, his bar had been a meeting ground for *El Grupo* who I learned had formed a tight-knit group in Cuenca and together were pushing the envelope in the Spanish art scene. The bar was empty, except for José Luis making the *mojito* I had mistakenly ordered. He had disappeared for twenty minutes, ostensibly to go pick the mint from his outdoor *terraza.* When he returned with a cigarette hanging from his lips, I watched him crush the mint and then proceed to pour a third of a cup of sugar into the drink.

"Like I said, what do you have to do with those assholes?" José Luis practically growled then laughed as he stirred the drink. He didn't appear that interested in my answers—he seemed to get more pleasure out of teasing me than hearing my response.

So I lied. "I am studying them for my thesis."

"Your thesis? You must have nothing else worthwhile to do if you are studying them. What, in America you have finished with Picasso?"

"Do you not like their work?"

"Like their work? *Señorita*, I have nothing to say about any of these assholes and their work. Their paintings hang on walls, but I knew those assholes and they've all left me. Rotting in this stupid bar while their stupid canvases hang on the walls of the Prado and museums in Frankfurt and Paris. Fuck them. You know, fuck them, and fuck Spain."

I had no idea where this conversation was going or what José Luis meant. I was grateful for Omar's help in referring me to someone who knew and could speak of anything related to my father, but I questioned how much help this man would be. He appeared to be drunk and his insults were increasingly slurred. The *mojito* sat untouched in front of me.

"I tell you, you should forget about all of them. There are more important things than art. What is art anyway!?"

I was in no mood to get into a philosophical conversation with a drunk Spanish bar man about the meaning and value of art. I was hungry and tired and just wanted a good lead on my father. And now, I was stuck at this bar with not even a place to stay the night. Maybe José Luis would give me more information when he sobered up, but this was pointless. I laid out 400 *pesetas* and thanked José Luis, then ducked out mumbling I'd be back soon. He barely noticed as I left.

Fuck, I thought. *My only lead in Cuenca is a mean drunkard.*

Chapter 7

It was evening by now. I'd been wandering around the old town for hours, ducking in and out of tourist shops selling honey and expensive Manchego, hoping to find a place to sleep for the night. I tried every hotel in the *Casco Antiguo*. But the hotels in the old town were out of my price range. There was a beautiful hostel called *La Posada* but the nice lady there told me they were booked for the next week. *Shit.* I should have done a better job planning this, I thought. My bag was getting heavy on my shoulders and my stomach was growling.

Wasted from the day, I stopped into a small storefront to buy some fruit and cheese to tide me over until I could find a place to stay for the night. A collection of old women gathered around the glass case filled to the brim with various types of sausages, cheese, and ham.

"*Claro, claro,*" they almost shouted.

"... She's lost her leg to the diabetes. They cut it off. Cut it off!" The women answered varying shouts of "*pobrecilla*" in reply.

"After everything, to lose a leg like that. I mean, cancer is one thing—but to lose a leg!"

All but one of them carried a cane. They were short and squat, with bad hairdos. Except for one. She appeared about their age, but held herself like a woman at the peak of her strength, not like someone who was seventy or eighty years old. The other ladies mostly donned permed and colored helmets, but her natural silver hair was wound in a perfect bun. She stood about six inches taller than the rest, and wore a bright red coat over a white cotton wraparound apron.

Then she spoke. "*Bueno,*" she said almost in a whisper, "If you hear of anyone looking for a place…I need to find a renter for my apartment."

"Did that last one leave already?"

"*Claro*, he's been gone a week now. And well, it wouldn't matter but with gas so expensive, who can afford not to work?"

"*Hombre*," they agreed.

The white-haired lady behind the counter looked up and asked me forcefully but nicely, "What can I do for you, *chica*? What do you need?"

"*Buenas tardes*," I said awkwardly. I looked at the woman with the silver hair who had mentioned needing someone to rent her apartment and took a deep breath, then blurted out in my best Spanish:

"I am looking for a place to stay tonight." My Spanish was still rough, though they appeared to understand me.

"What are you, American?" The white-haired lady behind the counter asked me, forcefully but not unkindly.

"Yes, I am from California."

"*¡Ah, California!*" The ladies exclaimed in unison.

"Where, San Francisco?" Asked the shopkeeper excitedly. "*Que maravilla…*"

"No, actually, I'm from Los Angeles."

"*¡Ah, Los Angeles!*" Again, the ladies commented.

"Yes, have you been there?" I asked the group.

"*¡Baywatch!*" They exclaimed. I nodded. I hoped the inquisition was over. Indeed, it appeared I had passed the test.

"Look no further, *guapa*, María del Carmen was just telling us how she was looking for someone to rent her little apartment."

The woman with the silver bun stepped forward and looked me over. I noticed how straight her spine was, and how broad her shoulders were. Her face was different too; her cheeks had a ruddy color to them, and while the lines of age had marked her, her green-grey eyes gave her a timeless look.

"Eh," she nodded towards me, "you need a room?"

"Good evening, *Señora.* Yes, I am looking for a place to stay for a few days."

"*Que yo no soy ninguna Señora*!" She and the other ladies laughed.

"Oh, okay," I stuttered, clearly not in on the joke.

"Don't worry, *guapa*," piped in the white-haired shopkeeper. "María del Carmen just isn't very formal. That's why we call her by her full name, to tease her. *¿Eh Carmen*?" The jolly shopkeeper gave a hearty laugh and winked at the poised lady with the white apron and a silver bun.

"*Bueno, guapa*, it's just a one-room apartment. But if you like, come and see it right now," she said, turning towards the street. I followed her out of the store dumbly, unsure of what to say or do next.

The shop woman called out behind us, "No one keeps a home like María del Carmen! You are in good hands, *niña*! They don't make women like this in the United States!"

I had no idea what to say in Spanish as the woman led me across the street, but I rejoiced at my luck. We passed through a large *portal*, and up four flights of stairs to the apartment. As we climbed the stairs in silence, we landed at a little brown door at the top of the stairwell. She unlocked the door with pride. Her hand on the door handle, she said,

"It's nothing other-worldly, but it has something special. I will clean it each day while you are here. I used to clean rooms at the *Posada*, but now it's just this one."

Then she opened the door. I could hardly contain myself. The room was breathtaking. It had vistas of the valley below and the mountains and river beyond. The floors were laid with terracotta tiles, and the kitchen counter was made of white marble. There was a double bed, a dresser, an empty bookshelf, and table and chairs. It was simple, but exactly what I needed. And there, on the wall, like a signpost, like a signal fire, was a lithograph. The woman gave me a moment to take it in.

"Is that...one of the painters from *El Grupo*?"

"*Pues, sí*" she responded, with a look of satisfaction. "How do you know about *El Grupo* ?"

"Every art student knows of *El Grupo*!" I feigned confidence then immediately changed the subject. I wasn't ready to reveal who I had come looking for to this kind stranger.

"I'm sorry, I forgot to even tell you my name. I'm Izzy."

"Izzy? That's a strange name."

"It comes from Isabel."

"Ah, Isabel. Of course."

"I'm a painter from the United States. I'm studying in Europe right now. What did you say your name was?"

"My name is María del Carmen Altamira León. They call me 'Carmen.' Nice to meet you," she said.

"The room is wonderful. I'll take it." Carmen laughed heartily.

Without hesitation I handed over enough *pesetas* for a week's stay. Carmen showed me how the stove and gas heating worked, explained she would check on me daily, and suggested I buy my bread at the shop we'd just met at. As she was leaving, Carmen stopped to look me up and down, but she said nothing. I was getting used to being looked at funny in Spain. But I didn't care, I was overjoyed. After a long day, I was relieved to have found a place to stay with a nice old lady to look after me.

Chapter 8

THE NEXT MORNING I was up early. I didn't want to waste any time in learning about my father's whereabouts. I left the cool calm of the apartment I'd rented from Carmen and let myself out of the building I would call home for a few days, the heavy black door slamming shut behind me. I headed up to the *Plaza Mayor*, around the side of the cathedral to a narrow cobblestone pathway which climbed the back of the cathedral and then sloped down in steep descent towards the river below. I stopped at a bar nestled behind the cathedral to have some breakfast and establish my plan. I still felt extremely foreign in this place, but I was starting to get the hang of it. I ordered a *café con leche* and two slices of toast with a side of butter and jam. The bar man was as gruff as José Luis had been, but at least was sober and did not yell at me. As I ate breakfast, I wrote out what I knew so far: *El Grupo* had gotten their start thanks to a wealthy patron of the arts, Federico Zorita. The group was unofficially led by Alejandro Soto. Most of the painters had lived in Cuenca for at least twenty years but since the late eighties and nineties, many had spread out to Madrid or Bilbao and Paris. Soto had died several years earlier, but Regalado, Torres, and Molina were still alive. In addition to José Luis, I guessed others in this town must know at least one of them. Maybe the museums had contacts? Carmen had an *El Grupo* painting, so there must be a connection there, though I would wait to ask her for fear of putting off the landlady too quickly. The shopkeepers might know as well, but I decided the museum was my best bet. There, I would be welcome and it would not be out of the ordinary to ask about the whereabouts of these painters.

After breakfast I made my way to Cuenca's Museum of Abstract Art. Painters from *El Grupo* had founded the museum and many of the group's paintings reportedly hung there; they had a library as well. The museum was cut into the hill and appeared to be jutting ninety degrees out of the mountain. Dozens of these hanging houses or *casas colgadas* lined the mountainside of the old town. I realized now that even the room I had rented from Carmen must have been part of a *casa colgada*. The effect of the hanging houses, particularly in the museum, was the appearance that enormous, sculpted rocks were suspended in mid-air all around you as if you were in a kind of mountainside fun house. Instead of mirrors reflecting strange images back to you, the rocks made all kinds of fantastical shapes.

The museum had a respectable collection. It held works by artists I had never even heard of. But the work was serious—you could tell it had its place in the Spanish history books. In the lobby, I scanned the names of the artists represented here: Molina, Rojas, Toset, Torres, Soto, Regalado. There they were. Somewhere among them, my father, hanging on the fourth floor! I wondered if I could identify my father by his painting alone—I still had no name to go on. Did painting style travel through bloodlines and DNA? Could I identify him by brushstrokes that felt like my own?

The bulk of the paintings were hung at the end of a long hall laid with Saltillo tiles. As I approached them, I drank in the meaning of being here, among these paintings, among their histories. I had made it. Against my mother's wishes and twenty years of living clueless to my roots, I had made it. A little wooden window frame just large enough to sit in was cut into the wall, opposite a large canvas. I hopped up and installed myself there. The paintings were not perfect like a Monet or Degas. But you could see the group playing with form and textures in ways that must have been ahead of their time. Their frames held ghoulish shapes and disturbing splatters across the canvas. They were not cubist like Picasso, not as unfettered as Pollack. I didn't like all the paintings. But each one was disturbing in its own way, which I knew meant something. So among them was my blood. Among them was my root. *No wonder the bulls sent my mother over the edge.*

"The work is good, no?"

I turned, shaken to see where these Spanish-accented English words had come from.

"—I'm sorry?"

"*El Grupo.* Molina. Regalado. Soto. Their work is very powerful."

"Yeah…yes it is." I shook off my reverie and jumped down off the window ledge. I felt suddenly like a goofy American without manners. *Who sits on window ledges in museums?* I reprimanded myself.

"I'm Rafael, I work here at the museum. I saw you were spending time with their work. Is there something I can help you with?"

"Oh, no, I'm just looking"—then, I changed my mind. I decided this was my chance. "But actually, I'm here studying *El Grupo.*"

"*¡El Grupo! ¡Vaya, que bien!* We rarely have Americans study Spanish modernists. And except for Soto, *El Grupo* rarely gets the attention it should. What luck to meet you. Can I answer any questions for you?"

"You have no idea. My name is—" I nearly introduced myself as Izzy, then changed my mind and decided to go with my given name, not the nickname I'd carried for so long.

"My name is Isabel. Good to meet you."

"And I'm Rafael, Associate Curator here at the museum. Pleased to meet you."

We shook hands and turned to look again at the room of paintings, one of which my father's hand had created. Rafael and I talked about the paintings till it was time to close the museum for lunch. He asked me to wait for him to close up, and invited me to join him for a beer.

Rafael was a lanky Spanish intellectual, who soon told me he had only recently moved out from under his mother's roof, at the age of 29 (which, Carmen later assured me was quite normal in Spain). Despite his boyish, awkward manner, the more time I spent with Rafael, the more I liked him. As we sat at a table in the *Plaza Mayor*, enjoying *croquetas* and *jamón*, I said to Rafael,

"You must tell me everything you know about the group. I've tried to do research on them, but I haven't found many clues about the painters on the Internet or in the libraries."

Rafael laughed and said, "Well if you don't mind me boring you, I can start from the beginning."

"You will not bore me! I promise."

"*Bueno. A ver...*" Rafael adjusted his glasses and settled into his chair. Around us, the *plaza* clattered with lunchtime activity. But all I heard were Rafael's words, outlining the first history lesson I'd ever had on my father. Rafael didn't know yet why I was so eager to learn about *El Grupo*, but he knew a ton, and I was grateful for his willingness to share.

I marveled at the stories I heard from Rafael. As I listened to him, I thought of my bulls again and how that small detail had set in motion the past four years of my life. We finished our beers and agreed to meet the next day at a place he called the *Fundación*.

I made the short walk back to the apartment, ready for a long siesta. *No wonder the bulls,* I laughed to myself. I was also in awe of the life I was witnessing around me. I was related—as in flesh and blood—to this place! The *plaza* was full of tables filled with people of all ages—twenty somethings, middle-aged men, even old ladies in polyester dresses and orthopedic shoes rocking babies in carriages while drinking beer and eating plates of blood red, thinly sliced Iberian ham.

As I made my way back to Carmen's apartment, I noticed a faint sense of contentedness lurking inside me. Spain was an easy place to love. *Now,* I thought, *if I can find my father, this dream will be complete.*

Chapter 9

THE *FUNDACIÓN* WAS a 17th century convent that a man named Andrés Padilla had filled with all the art his painter friends had given him through the years. He wrote their reviews and offered his services editing the programs for their exhibits. In turn, they paid him in paintings, or *cuadros,* as Rafael had instructed me they were called.

Rafael and I walked through the long halls that nuns, or *monjas*, had roamed in their robes for over a century—now these halls held the secrets of this band of painters my father had been a part of. It was one of the most beautiful museums I had ever seen. Rafael filled our visit with thrilling narrative:

"*Es importante*, if you want to understand this group, to understand the painters—who they learned from and kept company with. You have to understand that they were painting in Spain under Franco, after decades of oppression. These painters were taking risks—crazy risks, Isabel. This was the middle of pure *franquismo.* What they did, what they created was remarkable. But to people in Spain, recovering from the spell of fascism, it was hard to see. And the larger world was slow to recognize it, too. Do you know, there's a story that my boss told me…not long after the Museum of Abstract Art opened, when the museum could barely get a group of school kids to visit, the director invited the head of the Museum of Modern Art—"

"You mean MOMA, like New York MOMA?" I asked.

"Yes, that one, *exacto.* So to everyone's surprise, the director of MOMA accepts. And the staff, who'd spent months getting anyone to notice what this little group of painters in this small town called Cuenca was doing, were terrified how he would react. It would make or break their reputation. So anyway, the director of MOMA comes from New York, and he walks through the entire museum in absolute silence, and when he's done, he asks if he can walk through it again. And the museum staff, they're sweating from fear, maybe he hates it they are all thinking. But he tours it again in silence. And then again. And at the end of the third time through, he pauses and everyone is waiting to hear what he will say. When he finally spoke, he said, 'I believe this is the most beautiful museum I have ever seen.' And with that, the *Museo* was born. After that, people came from all over the world. Eventually even Spain caught on that they had something special here. *La joya de Cuenca.*"

Rafael told a mean story. I'd waited my whole life to hear about my father's origins. I soaked up every detail.

"Rafael—how did they end up here?"

"You mean in Cuenca?"

"Yes, why were they not in Barcelona or Madrid?"

"Mostly because Federico Zorita, a wealthy man who loved art and needed a way to spend his family's old money, loved Cuenca. He loved painting and he loved Cuenca, so he brought them together. That's why we're here, Isabel, that's why this museum is here."

"And what about now, where are they now?"

"Who, Zorita? Soto?"

"I dunno, any of them."

"Who knows. Spread to the ends of the earth I suppose."

"So you have no idea where even one of them is?"

For the first time since we'd met the day before, Rafael looked at me suspiciously, "Can I ask, Isabel…it is strange to have an American so interested in something like this group. It's not like Picasso or Chillida, who everyone is after. It's unusual. What has you so interested in this ragtag band of painters from Cuenca?"

I paused and looked at Rafael. I decided I needed an ally.

"Rafael, I…am not just here writing my thesis. Actually, I am not writing my thesis at all."

"You're not?"

"No. I'm sorry, I made that up. I am here because…because I believe…" just as I was about to utter the words, my mouth went dry and for the first time I felt emotion welling up inside my throat.

"Isabel, what is it?"

I took a deep breath.

"I believe one of the painters from *El Grupo* is my father."

Rafael's eyes grew wide and his mouth fell open. Then his brow furrowed and he looked at me seriously.

"*¿Es cierto*, Isabel?"

"*Sí*, it's true."

Rafael took a deep breath and held it for a moment, then let it go with the strongest expletive that exists in Spanish.

"*Me cago en dios*." (I later learned this translates roughly into "I shit on god," but I had a pretty good sense it was not a good thing when Rafael said it).

"Seriously?"

"Seriously. You see, I paint myself, and I always thought that the gift came from somewhere. But until recently, I didn't know who my father was…"

For a moment Rafael went quiet as he considered the implications of my being the forgotten daughter of *El Grupo*. Then suddenly, his eyes lit up.

"Wait, Isabel, where did you say you were staying?"

"Just down the street, I rented a little studio from a nice old lady I met at the local market."

"Yeah, that's what I mean. *Which* nice old lady?"

"María del Carmen...she goes by Carmen. I don't know much else about her but she seems really—"

"*Coño*…Isabel, you don't know who María del Carmen is? Isabel, *que buena suerte.* What luck. You've landed at the honorary home and hearth of *El Grupo.*"

Chapter 10

You do not know that birthing you nearly killed me. You do not know this, because I've never softened enough to tell you. You knew, in a way, you knew, because though I loved you, as all mothers love their daughters, I could not prize you and hold you and claim you, utterly as a part of my being. (For I would have also had to admit you were part of him—part man/part burro*/part gypsy/ part drunk/part artist/part faraway dream who I could never claim). To claim you would be to touch again the life that I lived so briefly—was it 4 months or 4 days or 4 minutes? I really couldn't say. Did we make love 40 times or 4? Or none at all? Without you, I could have called it a dream. It would have made for fantastic stories to tell to friends about a summer spent in Spain. I could have claimed my part. How I belonged to that inner circle. How they doted upon me and fed me* copas *and* camarones *while we laughed from night into light of morning. I could have brought home photos of cobblestones and drooping Gothic creatures that hung from churches there. Back home I could have flirted with Spanish boys visiting from abroad. I could have told them my stories and they would have called me 'worldly'.*

Instead, I chose something else. Instead, I took his love 4 times or 40 and you were born. Your birth was proof of my betrayal; how could I claim you the way that babies must be claimed? How could I fawn or adore or call you pet names, put your finger paintings above my desk? How could I claim the one who came out of him, killed her, and silenced me?

In art school I studied the classic American painters like John Singer Sargent. I loved his realism, the nobility he gave to his subjects in their upright portraits. But the art blowing up outside the walls of my stuffy east coast art school was the stuff of Cindy Sherman, Willem De Kooning and Robert Rauschenberg. I took twice weekly pilgrimages to the New York Met. I'd often go just to be with one of Rothko's monolith tableaus. I'd sit on the bench and converse with it silently as if meeting an old friend. I was young and naïve, untouched by the cynicism and materialism of the art world. I burned up for these works and took copious notes at every new exhibit I went to. Somewhere those notes are buried and with them, another woman—a young woman—you would not recognize. So how then did I end up, as my father would say, "like so"? How did I become this shell of a woman, my once long blond curls, now grey, cropped short, with bifocals and arthritis?

I have wasted 20 years of my life in a futile attempt to hide this story from you. It's time you heard this story. It's time I confessed to you how I got here, why you were implicated in a history you did not play a part in. That young woman I used to be, I can hardly see her now, but she was a brave and lovely beast. I will not tell her story from my jaded perch here at my 42 years that feel much more like 62. I would not be partial or fair to her; for all her naïveté, she was lovely.

You've asked me all your life to tell you this story. So listen closely, because I have spent your whole life trying to avoid it. But you've gone to Spain now and whatever I do not tell you, the cuadros *and shopkeepers will. So I will tell you. Here is my story, here is your story. Here is what happened in Cuenca in the summer of 1978.*

Cuenca, Spain 1978

They called her *la rubia* when they saw her. At the local market, at the *museo* in the Old Town where she frequented the cavernous library filled with the biographies of European and American painters. She stood out among the dark-haired Spaniards in this remote outpost. It was not like Madrid where American tourists had been in and out for years now. Cuenca may have caught the attention of Soto and his group of painters, but few outside Spain knew about it.

Rebecca had come here, like most of the painters, under the patronage of Federico Zorita—a hunchbacked cripple who had more money than he knew what to do with, and a love of abstract painting that gave him a way to spend his father's colonial pesos from the Philippine Islands. Zorita was a colleague of Rebecca's father at Harvard. He was hoping to open America's eyes to Spanish painters; there was no better way to start than inviting young apprentice curators like Rebecca. Federico Zorita had brought her here with only one demand:

"Study the art of these men," he had told her. "Spain needs their art—the world needs their art. The world will not take Spain seriously until it proves it can be more than Franco."

And so Rebecca had taken him up on his offer. Zorita himself came to Madrid to get her and deliver her by train to his beloved city, Cuenca. As their train pulled into the station, Zorita pointed to a woman in a white apron, her brownish-gray hair piled neatly into a bun:

"That woman there, she will look after you here. You will be in good hands with this woman…the best in the world...But you will not forget what I told you—Spain needs these painters, you won't forget?"

"I am grateful for the chance, Señor Zorita, you have my word."

"One more thing then" the half crippled man said, taking Rebecca's hand. "It may be difficult at first. The painters, they may not take you seriously, you may be lonely. So, *deja las cosas estar*, Rebecca. Let things come, let things unravel as they will, Rebecca—this is not America. Spaniards, we do things in a different way. Americans, you do many things well. But you are always pushing things. Just let things come as they will."

The young apprentice and her half-crippled patron stepped out onto the platform from the train.

"Carmen!" Zorita called out to the woman he'd pointed to from the train.

Rebecca and Zorita made a funny pair, him hunched over from his scoliosis, and her, tall and thin, like a little bird. She had green eyes, a small thin nose and thick, strawberry blonde hair, which in Spain made her an object of beauty and interest. She thought at first the Spaniards meant her ill will, but really they had seen so few blondes. And then she was American, too. At that time in Cuenca, no one had seen anyone like her. Her skin was so fair—"*blanca blanca*," as Carmen would say later.

Carmen made her way expertly through the slight crowd on the platform, her hands folded behind her back as she walked. When she'd made her way to where Zorita and Rebecca stood, she gave Zorita a strong embrace and a kiss on each cheek. Then she turned to the young woman he had brought from America and asked politely:

"Does she speak Spanish, Federico?"

"*¡Sí!*" burst out Rebecca, grateful she had understood the woman's request.

Zorita and Carmen laughed. "She is a good one, Carmen, I think you will like her very much."

Carmen leaned in to give Rebecca a kiss on each cheek, as she had done to Zorita.

"I am Carmen. Welcome to Cuenca. You must be hungry—are you hungry?"

"*¡Sí!*" Rebecca replied again.

Zorita and Carmen laughed again. "I think we will get along fine, Federico," said Carmen. "Here, Rebecca, give me your bag, the taxi is waiting."

The taxi made its way from the train station through a modern section of town, then climbed a steep, winding cobblestone hill up to a four-story apartment building along the main artery of the *Casco Antiguo* of Cuenca. Rebecca had watched in stunned silence as they passed the brightly colored apartment buildings with their wrought iron verandas. Gas street lamps hung from the sides of the buildings. Except for the cars, it looked to Rebecca as though she'd stepped back 200 years or fallen into another universe, very far from the one she'd always known. As they exited the taxi, Carmen must have noticed the young woman's eyes growing wide.

"Spain is a little...behind—"

"—It's beautiful" said Rebecca.

"Yes, Cuenca is a beautiful place. You will have much time to accustom yourself."

Carmen paid the taxi and, again taking Rebecca's bag from her, led the girl to a big black door with a shiny brass knob as large as Rebecca's hand. She took a set of keys from her apron pocket, then unlocked the door and pushed it open forcefully.

"*Pasa*" she prodded Rebecca.

Carmen led Rebecca up the stairs. The wooden steps creaked as they went, but they shined as brightly as the brass knob had. A lamp hung from the middle of the stairwell and turned off periodically as they made their way up the stairs. A short old woman with fat arms and a floral apron stood sweeping at her doorway on the second floor, watching as Carmen led Rebecca up the stairs.

"*Muy buenas, Doña Lupe*" Carmen said as they went. The old woman replied with a perfunctory "*Buenas*" but seemed more interested in Rebecca than in greeting Carmen.

Four flights of stairs led almost to the top of the stairwell to an unusually small doorway. Carmen stopped and pointed to the little door—

"*Mi puerta.*" Then she got a sparkle in her eye and pointed up the last flight of stairs to another door. "*Tu puerta.*"

Carmen led Rebecca up to the apartment, pulled the keys from her apron pocket and unlocked the door to Rebecca's new home.

Years later, after Rebecca had messed up her relationship with Carmen, and broken her promise to Zorita, she'd come back to this room in her mind, over and over again. It was no more than 500 square feet—just a one-room apartment with a kitchenette and a tiny bathroom with a tub and a view of the mountains. But there was a kind of magic that hung from the walls—maybe it was what Carmen had put into it, maybe it was here from the day the building was built in the 1700s atop cliffs the Arabs had unsuccessfully attempted to scale for centuries. Yes, later, when Rebecca could never go back, she'd think of the arched rooftop with long wooden beams that crossed the ceiling, dividing the room in half. She'd remember the way the light filled up the room until the walls seemed like they had been starched white by Carmen's very hand. There were the terracotta tiles that Carmen had brought in from Córdoba and paid a *dineral* for. The old dresser and bookshelf Carmen had found on the street and refinished herself. The marble slab that she had put in as a kitchen countertop in the little *cocina americana* as Carmen had called it. The square window in the kitchen that looked out to the old Jewish quarter below and the cathedral above. How Rebecca would miss the way the cliffs were lit up at night, and how she'd just stare at their enormous cuts of rock in the distance, directly facing her at the window, like proud members of the *Guardia Civil*, keeping watch over the city of Cuenca.

Chapter 11

THE APARTMENT WAS humble, but it was the loveliest thing Rebecca had ever seen. Rose geraniums hung in clay pots in the windows.

Carmen offered a small concession. "I've never been to New York, I don't know what apartment buildings are like there, but I imagine it's different. I hope you like it here."

"*Señora*, I am very happy to be here, and the apartment is perfect."

"I am no Lady or Madame. Just call me Carmen."

"*Bueno*, Carmen…this is the most beautiful place I've ever been."

Carmen laughed and said, "It's true. I don't know what it is, but it has something special."

Zorita and Carmen were true to their word. Within hours after Rebecca's arrival, Carmen had cooked Rebecca the best meal she'd ever eaten, helped the girl unpack her bag, washed the very clothes on her back, and left a freshly made coffee cake "just in case," as Carmen had told her. As Rebecca lay down to sleep that night, she smiled to herself at how grateful she was for her father's insistence she consider Spain—most of her friends were stuck filing papers at some forgotten museum in Chicago or Atlanta. She could not wait to write to her father, telling him about everything she'd seen already on her first day and the woman whose rented apartment she'd be living in for the next four months. She thought her father would like very much to hear about Carmen. Since her mother had died, he'd always tried to bring women into their lives, usually with little success. But Rebecca had never seen an American woman like Carmen—the apron, the bun, the domestic world she seemed to master effortlessly—all this was entirely new to Rebecca.

Rebecca didn't know much about the woman, other than the fact that her husband, also a painter, was one of Soto's close friends. Carmen had told her this as they unpacked Rebecca's bag:

"*Sabes*, being the partner of a painter, you learn how artists work. How to support them. I don't know much about art, I am not an artist, I just understand what it takes to love one."

To that Rebecca did not know what to say, or even how she would reply if she had all the words in Spanish.

"*¿Es difícil*? Is it difficult to love an artist?" Rebecca said, cringing at her simple Spanish.

"It's what I know," replied Carmen, "but it's not for everyone."

It made sense to Rebecca; it took a certain type to study art but not make it, too. Carmen looked at Rebecca, as if assessing this recently arrived specimen.

"You're probably tired. What do you say, would you like to take a bath before dinner? You'll rest much better later. Would you like that?"

"I thought I might take one after dinner."

"*Qué va*, you should not take baths after you eat—you'll catch a cold!"

"Really? I've never heard that!"

"*Claro*, it interrupts your digestion. No no, better not wait till after dinner. You have plenty of time. Would you like me to lend you a robe, *niña*? I've got a brand new robe for you, just wait."

Carmen rushed out of the apartment to get Rebecca a robe to borrow. Rebecca was amazed at the generosity of this woman she'd only just met.

"*Aquí tienes.* You're going to look like a ghost in this white thing, but… You'll have a nice bath… The soap too I've got is very good. It's from Paris, from an herbalist there, and it's made with aloe vera. It's real soap, not that bath gel. You'll bathe and I'll bring you up a little fish stew. Do you know *marmitako*? And be sure to turn on the heat in the bathroom so you don't catch cold and so the paint won't crack. Pull that little cord to turn on the electricity. Okay?"

"Carmen, how can I thank you for all this?"

"*Qué va, no es ná…*But you know, somehow, I feel like I already know you. It's silly, but I have a sense of these things. I think we'll get along very well."

"Yes! I think so too!" Rebecca cried in agreement. The American girl's enthusiasm made Carmen laugh.

"Well then, let's not have this old lady keep you from your bath. I will bring the soup up in just a little and leave it on the stool by the door so I don't interrupt you. You can ring my bell if you need anything at all. You are in your home now. Alright?"

"*Gracias*, Carmen. *Gracias*."

Carmen leaned in and gave the girl a kiss on each cheek as she had done when they met at the train station and as she would do every time they met in the future. With her mother having passed away when she was young, this felt like a woman she could really get to know. While she prepared her bath, Rebecca felt sure, something about this apartment, something about this woman made her feel very much at home. As nervous as she'd been to fly across the world to an unknown place, as anxious as she was to get to know Soto and his gang of painters, Rebecca felt as safe and cared for as she ever had. She could not wait to explore Cuenca; every last street, shop and cafe she would uncover. That night, Rebecca wrapped herself tightly in Carmen's soft sheets that smelled of lavender. Yes, this would be her best summer yet.

Chapter 12

WITHIN A FEW days, Rebecca had mapped out the entire town of Cuenca. She was an avid walker and until Soto returned from Paris, she had little else to do. *El monte*, Carmen said, is the best company.

Rebecca began each day with an orange juice and coffee cake in the *Plaza Mayor*, and then she set out for the hills that encircled Cuenca. She talked to them like a young child would, chirping and singing away at them happily, practicing her Spanish with them like silent language instructors.

Rebecca had never seen mountains like these. It was not their size—they had no pretensions of greatness. But their hills had been cut by the gods. Each tiny speck of limestone packed so tightly, then washed over with a million years of oceans and tears. And now they were like bodies, or poems each one, poking out from the mountain. These were not rocks nor hillsides, but enormous pieces of bone jutting this way and that. Sometimes on her morning walk she could almost see faces cut out of the stone. She could hear the ridges calling out to one another, laughing as the wind rolled around their edges and through the shrubs that grew out of the cracks.

"*¿Cómo te llamas?*" Rebecca would whisper out to them.

"*Yo me llamo Rebecca, soy hija única, soy de Nueva York.*" She'd rattle off everything she knew about herself, correcting her grammar beneath her breath. Then her chatter would get serious: "*Me siento muy libre aquí. ¿Sabes?* I feel very free here, you know?" She'd talk to the hills as Carmen talked to her—the same pauses and inflections in her monologue that she'd learned by listening to Carmen. *¿Sabes?* Carmen often ended her thoughts with a rhetorical "You know?" *¿Sabes?*

Rebecca's feet would crunch the gravel, her hands would flap at her sides, and her mouth would not stop moving—she had Spanish to practice and mountains to entertain. Even with the loneliness that sometimes set in, she felt free in Cuenca. With its rock formations, cobblestone streets and hanging houses. Rebecca had always thought she needed an ocean to be near—she couldn't imagine before coming to Cuenca being far from the Atlantic. And yet here, 200 miles from any sea, she felt completely at home, entirely fulfilled. She took in the morning light, the quiet of the early hours before the city began to hum. She would walk to the little cemetery atop the town or the other way, past the little stone church to the river below. It was as though the town welcomed her—let her into its secret homes, stories, and pathways. She had never felt that kind of admittance from any place before.

As Carmen would prepare one of the dozens of delicious dishes she cooked for Rebecca, she swore to the young American woman that Rebecca's sense of belonging was because her soul was *española*, through and through.

"*No eres americana,*" Carmen would say to her. "Nothing American about you. Your family must have come from *los judíos españoles*" the Jewish Spaniards, she insisted. Carmen loved the idea that Rebecca was really from a flock of Spanish Jews. She repeated this often and would describe the stories she'd heard about when the Jews lived peacefully alongside the Arabs and Christians in Cuenca.

"There down that road," Carmen would say as they sat by the kitchen window, "that was the Jewish quarter, *¿sabes?*"

Rebecca promised Carmen she would try to find out if she had Spanish roots. But either way, she was grateful for the way these mountains, this town let her into their secret mornings. She'd say in return to them, "Me? You're going to let me in?"

And the hillside, with its cuts of rock and homes hanging off the ridge over a cold green river below the hillside, just sighed a long and sweet, "*Sí.*"

Chapter 13

After a week of exploring Cuenca's hillsides and having a glass of wine in the *plaza* each afternoon, Rebecca began to feel the loneliness set in. Alejandro Soto had still not returned from Paris to meet her and begin their work together. There was no one to talk with at night, and she'd visited the town's museums a half dozen times already. Carmen had come around a few times; she cleaned the girl's apartment each day and would check in on her in the morning to see how she was doing. But Rebecca began to feel very alone, and had begun to wonder if she'd come to Cuenca in vain.

Carmen must have seen the change come over Rebecca. Her shoulders drooping, her step a little heavier. She met Rebecca in the stairs coming back from walking the dogs one morning.

"Your eyes are sad. What is wrong?"

Rebecca began to cry right then in the stairwell, her big brown eyes welling up. Someone had noticed, someone had seen her. She was grateful but it brought her walls of steel tumbling down. Rebecca's eyes filled with tears at the thought that Carmen had understood her sadness without her saying a word. "Stay right here," she ordered Rebecca.

Rebecca waited in the stairwell, as Carmen shut the dogs in her apartment. She could see Rebecca was in no mood to play with them. She returned with a handful of rosemary, a jar of honey and a bottle of milk.

"May I come in?" Rebecca nodded and Carmen took the keys to the apartment from her apron, unlocking the door quickly, then ushering Rebecca to sit in one of the large chairs around the table in her flat.

"You stay there," Carmen commanded.

Carmen went to work—her white apron was wrapped tightly around her hips like always. Carmen poured half a jug of milk into a pot, took a spoonful of honey from the jar and poured two teaspoons into the milk as it warmed on the stove. She stirred the milk and honey with a fresh stem of rosemary between the concerned glances she shot at Rebecca.

Rebecca did not like warm milk. But Carmen did not ask her and Rebecca did not have the words or strength to say anything, let alone in Spanish. Carmen started to speak to her as she stirred.

"*Sabes*—you know, it is hard to be alone in a new place, in a new country, *no es fácil*, it doesn't surprise me you are sad. Your family, your home, they are far away—and you know, this world isn't yours. Even if you feel at home here—it's a strange place."

Rebecca sat in her straight-backed chair beneath a large print by Carmen's husband, Regalado. She could see the green and pink hills outside of the kitchen window. All Rebecca could muster was a weak, "*Tienes razón.* It's true."

She was afraid to say more, for fear she'd start bawling. But she could say another "*Tienes razón.*" and she repeated it softly between Carmen's words of support.

Carmen knew the girl could not yet express herself, nor likely understand all of what she was saying. So she spoke slowly and tried to reassure her.

"*Es difícil—y Cuenca, es muy especial. La gente*...they don't understand who you are or where you are from. Cuenca is not like Madrid, you know, people here don't understand. But you are here to learn, and you know already a lot, you know very much. You are smart and you can watch, listen, and learn from these artists, that is why you are here. Besides, Soto will be here next week, and with that, your lessons will begin."

Carmen poured the warmed milk into a white ceramic bowl. "Here, drink. It will warm you—you just got a little cold in the stomach. You have to stay warm here, we are very high up in Cuenca, you know. It gets cold and you must keep warm."

Rebecca took the bowl in her hands while Carmen watched like a protective mother bear. Carmen sat on the edge of the bed as she tucked the covers around Rebecca, who lay propped up against pillows, at Carmen's insistence.

"*Sí, sí, eso es,*" she repeated to Rebecca, softly.

Rebecca sipped from the bowl slowly, it was the best warm milk she had ever had. Sweet and not too hot. She felt it go down her throat and fill her sad stomach.

"Carmen...can we do this again sometime? Even if I'm not sick?"

Carmen broke into a peal of laughter. "*Niña*, whenever you like."

This was how their friendship began. A 54-year-old Basque woman and a 20-year-old New Yorker. Over a bowl of warmed milk. From then on, every afternoon at three, after lunch, before Carmen took her siesta and before Rebecca went back to work on her research, Carmen would walk up the stairs to Rebecca's apartment and the two women would chat for a half hour in the stairwell over tea and the whole-grain digestive biscuits that Carmen swore by.

Carmen would ask how Rebecca was doing and then Carmen would tell her stories from her life in Cuenca or San Sebastián. She would describe working in her parents' bar; running to the dock to buy the day's fish; and later, the fish shop she'd had in San Sebastián; her weekend trips to watch jazzmen in France; the fishing supplies she'd hidden beneath her car seat and traded for contraband at the border; leaving San Sebastián for Cuenca; and the first apartment she had had with Regalado in Bilbao; how poor they were and still how they would go see movies each week to fill them up with inspiration.

On Wednesdays, Rebecca would join Carmen for her weekly trip to the fish market in the city center.

"*Niña*," Carmen would counsel Rebecca, "I only buy fish on Wednesdays. It's the only day to buy fish. See, fish comes in fresh Wednesday and then again on Friday, but Friday's catch is never as good. Whatever you do, never buy fish on a Monday—it will have sat all weekend. Since we moved to Cuenca, I go every Wednesday. I go in the morning, after walking the dogs early. I only buy from one shop here, the others, they all freeze their fish and it tastes like cardboard or I-don't-know-what."

Carmen and Rebecca would walk down the hill arm in arm like a pair of old ladies, then take the bus back to get the fish in the fridge quickly. Sometimes they walked behind the cathedral and then down the stairs past a little artisan shop where they sold sculptures and bowls made by local artists.

Carmen would say, "Nothing serious, not like the museum, but sweet little things."

Other times they would take the bridge behind the cathedral and cross over to the ancient Monastery of San Pablo, then down the hill right into town. Rebecca was the only one Carmen ever let go with her.

"Don't get me wrong, I love *Doña* Amparo or Guadalupe, but… I like going to my fish shop by myself. You, *niña*, are the exception." Carmen smiled at Rebecca affectionately and Rebecca squeezed Carmen's arm tightly.

"And you, Carmen, are also the exception."

The fishmonger went by the name José Manuel. But he was Basque like Carmen and she called him by the Basque word for fisherman: *Arrantzale*.

"From *Gipuzkoa*. So he knows about fish. Us *vascos*, we know about fish, *¿sabes*?" Carmen would say each time to Rebecca as they entered the store. Carmen and Arrantzale would call out to each other in their native tongue:

"*¡Arratsalde on!* Good day!"

Arrantzale's shop had three enormous steel tables with raised edges. Each morning, he'd cover them with ice and then display the best fish in town. Carmen would enumerate the benefits of Arrantzale's fish often, her hands animating the movements of the fish in different seas:

"He never buys fish from the Mediterranean, or Africa. Never, never." At mention of the other, lesser seas where fish might be found, Carmen would tsk her tongue in disapproval and say:

"That's why his fish is so expensive. The other ladies in town, they don't understand why it costs a *dineral* to buy it there, but it's because the fish from the Cantabrian Sea are much better than the fish from Africa or Thailand. The Basque sea, you know, in the north is very strong—the current makes it hard for the fish to swim, they have to fight against every wave, they have to swim harder. So it makes them stronger, and they have a better texture—not flaccid like the fish from Africa or who-knows-where. Also, because the water is saltier in the north, and there are more minerals in the water, the fish come out tasting better. I am telling you, there's nothing like the *merluza* and *bacalao* from the north—it makes me think of my homeland, we had fresh fish every day there, *hombre*!"

He was not the friendliest shopkeeper in town. But when the *merluza* was good, or when the baby squid had come in fresh, or when the oysters were ready—Arrantzale knew. And he'd call Carmen and say, "María del Carmen, whatever plans you may have, you have to come today, you'll die for these *chipirones. Están que te mueres, Carmen.*" Or he'd call just to say, "Don't bother coming today, there's nothing but crap coming out of the sea."

Rebecca was learning, as Zorita had promised she would. Not from Soto, but from this *ama de casa*, what Americans called a "housewife."

Chapter 14

TWO WEEKS AFTER Rebecca's arrival, just as Carmen had promised, Alejandro Soto finally returned from Paris. Carmen rushed up to tell Rebecca as soon as she had heard.

"Soto is back. I'll invite him for lunch tomorrow so you can meet him—he loves my *salsa verde*. Tomorrow, at one o'clock—is it good for you?"

Rebecca nodded eagerly. "Thank you Carmen!"

"Regalado will be there too, so you can meet him finally. And you can see our apartment—you have not seen it yet. I must go buy fish tomorrow first thing," Carmen said, as she ran down the stairs to her apartment with an excitement Rebecca had not yet seen in her step.

"Tomorrow, one o'clock," Carmen repeated. "*Nos vemos*!"

Rebecca's heart was racing. This was the start to her work in Cuenca. Soto was the only one of Cuenca's painters who had reached international stardom. Soto's paintings had the energy and emotion of Picasso combined with the stark modernism of de Kooning. He painted big and bold, with lots of blacks and grays slapped across the canvas. He wasn't necessarily the best, but he was the one Spain had been waiting for—the one who would show the world it was modern too, that Franco hadn't been able to suppress that. Of all the painters who had set up shop in Cuenca, Soto was the first to be summoned there by Zorita. Soto agreed that Cuenca had something Paris or Madrid could not offer: Stunning natural beauty and an inexpensive price tag. Soto could set up a studio overlooking the hills and river valley for a fraction of what it was costing him on Paris' left bank. And, because Cuenca was a forgotten corner, he could paint in peace without gallery owners and art students knocking at his door all day.

Rebecca had waited anxiously for Soto's return. Her research, her reason for being, her reason for coming to Cuenca depended on his resources and support. With Zorita traveling in Rome till July, Soto was her only contact to begin her work—and she needed his support to get the other painters to open up to her. They were still skeptical of the outside world, particularly Americans—and her sex did not help her.

But now that would all change with Soto. Zorita had promised her Soto would teach her everything the Spanish modernists had to teach. Rebecca was ready.

The next day Rebecca was too nervous to go out for her morning walk. She paced around the apartment, unable to relax or focus on anything but the upcoming lunch with Soto. She could hear Carmen coming and going hurriedly, likely cleaning the house from top to bottom and retrieving the fish she'd ordered.

By 11am, Rebecca could smell the garlic wafting up from Carmen's kitchen. She realized, too, that she'd finally get to see Carmen and Regalado's home, something she'd been curious about since her arrival. Could it really be she'd only been here just a couple of weeks, she wondered. Already, the walls of Carmen's apartment felt like home, already she knew the streets by heart and many of the shopkeepers' names: Esperanza and Milagros from the market on *Calle Alfonso VIII,* María Jesús from the cheese and wine shop, Rodrigo from the bicycle and *moto* shop, Inmaculada from the pharmacy, and Señor Muñoz from the *Caja de Ahorros*, where Carmen had helped Rebecca set up a bank account. Yes, Rebecca had been introduced to everyone but the painters she'd come to study. Rebecca admonished herself for being so critical—*Today it begins*, she thought, *just stay positive and do like Zorita told you—don't push, everything in its time.*

At 1pm, Rebecca descended to Carmen's flat, one story below the apartment. She wore jeans and the white linen blouse that Carmen had liked so much when they were unpacking Rebecca's things. Her hair hung down around her shoulders and she'd been playing with it nervously all morning while she paced. She carried the bottle of wine from María Jesús she'd bought the day before to offer Carmen. The dogs heard her first and she could hear their heavy barking from somewhere in the flat.

"*Voy, voy*" called out Carmen several times, each time getting closer to the door amid the cacophony of her two barking dogs. The door swung open and Carmen stood through the tiny entry way several stairs below Rebecca.

"Well! Those dogs, those rascals! How are you? You're beautiful, look at you! That blouse enchants me, I could eat you up! No sad eyes today…well, maybe a little nervous, eh?"

Carmen was radiant, thought Rebecca. Even in her plain white apron, she was like no other woman Rebecca had ever known. She was three times Rebecca's age yet she seemed to have more energy than Rebecca had ever had in her entire life. Her cheeks were flushed pink and a wisp of graying hair fell from her otherwise perfectly-coiffed bun.

"Come in, come in, I don't want my whisky cake to burn. It's Rego's favorite. Come, come," Carmen entreated. Carmen stepped back to make way for Rebecca to enter into the apartment. Beyond the stairs that led to the hallway, was a large living room. Each wall had a large, brightly covered canvas, mostly Regalado's work from what Rebecca could tell, but there were others too; a Soto, a piece by Basque sculptor Chillida. Rebecca recognized several pieces instantly. A large wooden table held several stacks of art books. Behind the table, three wide-open windows held overflowing pots of rose geraniums and looked down to *Calle Alfonso VIII* below.

Rebecca looked around her carefully—she did not want to intrude, but she could not stop herself from taking in each detail.

"Carmen, it's beautiful. *No hay palabras.*"

"*Ah sí, ¿te gusta*? I keep it very simple, Rego wants to have more things, he says it is too minimal, but this is how I like it...*Venga, ¡vamos!* That whisky cake is calling me."

Carmen leapt at a quick pace down a hallway and then down a flight of stairs into the kitchen. Rebecca followed, taken by the woman's energy and home. By the time Rebecca had gotten halfway down the stairs, Carmen had already removed her creation from the oven and was tending to it. The entire house smelled like sweet, warm cake.

The kitchen was small, but an enormous window looked out to the hillside—the same view Rebecca had in her kitchen upstairs: Cuenca's dry but verdant cliffs, dotted with black pines, cork oak trees, and miles of sweet rosemary shrubs, jutting every which way along the hillside. Opposite the window was a ceiling to floor set of shelves that held jars of honey, porcelain jars marked "rice," "beans," "flour," and tins of *bonito.* Along one side of the kitchen was Carmen's half-fridge and the main counter and sink. The counter was made of the same marble that covered the counter in Rebecca's apartment. In the middle of the kitchen, a table was set with a green and white checked tablecloth; one of Esperanza's delicious loaves of bread sat in the middle of the table. Carmen maneuvered gracefully from the stove to the oven to the fridge. She moved so fluidly, so comfortably, so efficiently, it seemed she walked on her toes, thought Rebecca.

"What do you think?" asked Carmen.

"You have a very beautiful home. It brings me happiness to see it—"

Carmen laughed, "Ay Rebecca, you speak Spanish like a retarded cow."

"I am sorry, it is true, it is hard for me."

"Oh, do not worry, by the time you leave here you will be speaking like you were born here. And who am I to talk—I can't speak any English at all!"

"Is Soto coming?" Rebecca asked nervously.

"Clearly yes, he is coming with Rego. But first, I have to make the soup."

"Can I help you?" Rebecca always offered to help Carmen but Carmen would have none of it. So instead, Carmen cooked and narrated her instructions for Rebecca:

"Garlic soup, we're making. I saved this loaf of bread from yesterday. You cut it up like this, in little slices, little bits. Then, you take a pan and add oil and garlic. Lots of garlic. And the garlic has to brown. Once it's browned, you throw in all the bread. And you stir it and stir it around, so it soaks up all the oil. The bread has to be, like this, look. Broken up, see, like that, like that. Like that. *¿Sabes?* Then, when it's mixed up really well, you add water. Do you see? You add a little water and let the bread cook. This is good for people who've had too much to drink, and old people…it's very soothing. Here, during Holy Week and that, the night of the drunks, in all the bars they serve garlic soup. And what's more, it's so cheap you can just give it away. *Sopa de ajo.*"

Nearly an hour later, after the garlic soup had been made and the prawns had chilled to perfection—and just as Carmen was about to give up on the two painters, they showed up. Their footsteps were heavy on the stairwell, their voices boomed through the apartment building till they reached the front door. Rebecca picked at her nails, her heart beat wildly in anticipation. Carmen lit the stove and poured the olive oil into a pan, swishing it around before throwing a garlic clove in.

"What hunger I have! These two *locos* take their time."

"Carmen!" A man's voice yelled from upstairs. "Carmen!"

"*Ay, sí*, we are in the kitchen."

Two sets of footsteps came pounding down the stairs. Alejandro Soto entered the kitchen first, Rebecca recognized him from the books Zorita had lent her. He was shorter than Rebecca had imagined, with a slight paunch. He had combed over his hair to hide the fact he had been balding since he was in his forties. His face was round, with sideburns running down his cheek bones.

"Carmen! How is my favorite beautiful little insect? The jewel of Cuenca! I have missed you!" Soto wrapped his arms around Carmen.

"*¡Hombre*! How are you?" Carmen greeted him, then gave him a kiss on each cheek as she'd done with Zorita at the train station two weeks before. Regalado followed behind Soto into the kitchen. He was the opposite of Soto—tall, thin, with a head full of shaggy brown hair. Like Soto he wore the usual painter's uniform: Worn jeans with paint spots and a ragged t-shirt with a pack of smokes in the breast pocket.

Neither man was particularly handsome—Regalado in particular had a strange, elongated face with crooked teeth and a knot in his Roman nose. And yet there was something very attractive about both men—and they looked very different than all the Spanish men she'd met up till now. The other men—Esperanza's husband, Señor Muñoz at the bank, they all were better looking with tall backs and broad shoulders. Regalado and Soto did not look like them, but their faces were more interesting, more playful.

Regalado greeted Carmen with a hand to her shoulder, and both men sat down at the table, continuing their conversation, talking loudly about some friend of Soto's. They did not acknowledge the young woman who sat quietly at one corner of the table Carmen had set.

The two men filled up the kitchen with their loud chatter and booming laughter till Carmen finally interrupted them. "Alejandro—this is Zorita's girl, the one who is staying with us for the summer."

"*Ah, sí*," Soto said, turning to get a look at Rebecca. "*Encantado*" he added, then turned back to talk with Regalado. Rebecca felt awkward and foreign amongst the three of them; she could not understand their dialogue since it moved much too quickly for her to keep up. Carmen gave Rebecca a wink as if to say, "Be patient." Rebecca thought of Zorita's advice not to push and tried to just listen to the conversation as best she could. Carmen opened a bottle of white wine and poured them each a glass. Regalado gulped it down.

"And how's the wine?" Carmen asked Regalado. It was the first time since they had arrived that the two had spoken to each other directly.

"Stupendous," replied Regalado. As he said it, Rebecca saw Regalado and Carmen look each other in the eyes. It only lasted a moment, but the connection between the two of them was palpable.

Soto tried it and agreed, "It's really good, delicious."

Carmen re-poured their wine and said to Rebecca, "There's a village that has the best wine in all of Cuenca—Caracenilla."

"The prawns are damned good too, Carmen," said Regalado as he peeled the skin off the shrimp, his fingers still covered in oil paints.

After appetizers of garlic soup and chilled prawns, Carmen served the best fish Rebecca had ever eaten. But the two painters could not be bothered with Rebecca—in fact, they almost seemed to ignore her, she thought.

The four of them sat around Carmen's kitchen table, and a light breeze came in through the window. Rebecca ate, tried to look polite and not let herself cry right then and there. "It is early yet," she told herself, "do not give up, not after one lunch." But it did sting, and Soto seemed particularly disinterested in her. Regalado at least offered to pour her wine and translated a few times over lunch. With Soto, she would have a harder job than she had imagined.

When they'd finished lunch and Carmen had gathered all the plates from the table and poured two glasses of whiskey, Rebecca did something she could have never imagined.

"Carmen, me too, please. I'll have some whiskey."

"*¡Ay, mi chica*! You sure?"

"I have to get this man's attention somehow, right?" Rebecca asked, looking squarely at Soto.

"*¡Bueno*! Give the girl some whiskey, Carmen," cried out Regalado.

Carmen obliged, though pouring Rebecca less than she had for the two painters.

When she was done, Rebecca held up her glass and said in a loud voice she barely recognized,

"To never having to hang your paintings over some housewife's couch." Without a moment's pause, she threw the whiskey down her throat and shuddered as it went down.

Regalado and Soto looked at Rebecca for a moment, unsure of what to say or do next. Rebecca prayed silently her bet would pay off. Then from Soto's mouth came a loud, booming,

"Please no or I'll shit on God!" Regalado and Soto raised their glasses to Rebecca and Regalado shouted,

"*¡Mucho gusto*, Rebecca!"

Carmen watched from the corner of the kitchen with a proud look on her face. She knew it would take an act of genius to make these chauvinists see a young woman for what she really was, and not just a silly whim of Zorita's. As the two men downed their whiskey, she winked at Rebecca in support.

Rebecca had gotten their attention. Now all she had to do was prove herself.

Chapter 15

THAT VERY AFTERNOON after the *siesta*, Soto invited Rebecca to come for a visit at his studio. There were two canyons and two rivers in Cuenca. Carmen's home hung over the *Júcar* river. Soto's was on the other side, above the *Huécar,* the cold water colored an almost fantastical green from the minerals that lined its riverbed. Carmen had told Rebecca that the side you wanted to be on was by the *Júcar*—it was quieter, the light was prettier, and most of all, Carmen swore up and down that all the fascists in town lived over the *Huécar.* You could not pay her, Carmen said, to live anywhere near those—here Carmen's speech would devolve into a litany of expletives in Spanish that Rebecca could not distinguish, *para nada.* Suffice to say, Carmen did not like fascists and did not prefer that side of the Old Town. But that was where Soto's studio was, and regardless of who his neighbors were, Rebecca was eager to spend some time with the painter.

Word of Rebecca's "performance" spread quickly among Cuenca's painters. Soto and Regalado were impressed by the girl's *cojones,* as they said. They admitted between themselves their expectations had been low. While they all loved Zorita, they also saw him like a crazy old uncle who was always trying to get you to try a new product or marketing scheme. They were doubtful—Soto in particular—of what a young college student from New York could offer. But Rebecca had earned Carmen's affections, which had gotten their attention.

Soto invited her that very afternoon of the whisky to his studio. She was young, yes, but she knew her art, and as they would later admit to her, she was not patronizing or affected like so many Americans who had come to Cuenca to check in on the little group of Spanish abstract painters.

Rebecca spent several hours in Soto's studio. They talked about Picasso, about Miró, about De Kooning. They did not discuss Franco, nor politics, or nationality—simply art, art, art. They sat at the unfinished oak table off to the side of his studio. Other than a dried sausage hanging from the ceiling, there wasn't much else in the little corner that functioned as his eating area. The table was perched in front of a pair of open windows that looked out over the canyon. Rebecca kept thinking about Carmen and how she'd be cursing Soto's fascist neighbors if she were here. But as far as Rebecca could see, the view of the Mediterranean hills was just as stunning as it was from Carmen's kitchen window.

Soto asked Rebecca nothing of her studies or her background. This was fine with Rebecca—she was here to learn about the painters and she was going to take every minute he'd give her to find out all she could. She wanted to know why he'd begun to work almost solely in blacks and grays.

"*¿Por qué tanto negro y gris*? Before you painted with much more color—even pastels, right?"

"I don't know, maybe colors do not fit how I feel anymore. As if they are false, too bright, too happy. You know?"

"Will you go back to color?"

"We'll see. Now that I am done having children, maybe not. I saw a lot of color when the babies were born...then it disappeared. It might be black and white like this for the rest of my fucking life. Who can say?" Soto took a cigarette from his shirt pocket and placed it unlit in his mouth.

"What about the other painters?" Rebecca asked.

"It's true: Javi Molina, Abel Toset, Gonzalo Torres, Eutiquio Salazar—they have worked with a lot of blacks and whites, too. Even in Cuenca where there are so many colors; maybe it is Spain, maybe it's the forty years of brutal dictatorship we lived through, I don't know. I just feel like black is much more interesting than red anymore. We did red, Picasso, Rothko and all the others, they did it."

"You want to explore black."

"Yes," answered Soto, "I want to explore black. I like black very much," he said with a smile.

"Have you heard of *El duende*, Rebecca?"

Rebecca nodded. "'*The duende is not in the throat; the duende climbs up inside you, from the soles of the feet…*'" Soto laughed as Rebecca quoted the beloved Spanish poet's description of music and art with a deep, dark soul.

"Yes! Lorca, you know him!" Soto clapped his hands together, satisfied with the knowledge of his young apprentice.

"Magnificent. How wonderful you know him and *el duende*… that demonic spirit that gets inside of the artist…that turns everything upside down…that battle inside us to release the dark spirit into the world…So then you will understand my interest in black… in darkness." Soto paused and then laughed at himself.

"We are such assholes, we painters."

"No, no, it's not true," assured Rebecca.

"Yes, yes we are. And that goes for you too, *rubia*, even if you don't paint—you study this crap, it makes us all pretentious cunts."

"*Bueno*, Rebecca" he said as he lit the cigarette that had been hanging from his mouth.

"I know you've come because Zorita wants to make the whole world know about the wonder and magic of Spain's painters. I don't know if we have anything to offer them—we're just doing what we have to do as artists. It might not be anything special or interesting. So what do you want to do while you're here? What am I supposed to do with you?"

Rebecca had had her first chance to get Soto's attention in Carmen's kitchen. She'd used the whiskey to win that battle. Here was her second chance—she felt her heart quicken as it had just before Soto and Regalado had appeared in Carmen's kitchen hours earlier. Rebecca looked at Soto carefully—whatever she said to him here would make the rounds among the others; she had to be real and be honest, and she had to be quick about it.

"See that *chorizo* hanging from the wall there, Alejandro?"

"*Claro*, that's how I eat after my wife's gone to bed. What about it?"

"You painters here in Cuenca, you guys are like that sausage. Full of hot pepper and wrapped tightly in your little casing. If you want someone to know what you're about, if you don't want to just hang from a nail on the wall in a little town in Spain, you have to take it down, remove the casing and let people have a taste."

"But we don't give a shit about what anyone thinks of our *chorizo*."

"I know—and in the end, it does not matter what they think. But you also do not want your work to sit in an attic somewhere that was made to cure ham. Is it true?"

Soto nodded. "*Joder, guapa*, you've got some balls."

"No, not at all. I'm just trying to show you the value in my being here. It's to help you. I have much more to learn than I could ever teach you. But if you will trust me, I will do what I can to show the world what you are doing in Cuenca. It matters, it does."

"Okay, between the whiskey, the *chorizo*, and *el duende*, you have proven yourself, *rubia*. But what do you want to do here? Just watch me paint?"

"No."

"Then what?"

"Let me in."

"Let you in? Where?"

"Let me watch you and the others, let me join your world for a few months. Let me into your studios, put up with my questions, do not treat me like some project Zorita has thrown in your lap."

Soto took a last drag on his cigarette, then extinguished it on the window sill.

"Okay. But, *guapa*...do not disappoint me. I will tell the others."

Soto bid Rebecca to come to Jovi the next night at midnight. "That's where we meet on Thursdays after our women have gone to bed. I'll make the introduction. We'll see what we can do."

Rebecca did as Soto had asked of her. She went to Jovi at midnight to be introduced to the other painters. She paid close attention to her dress as she readied herself to go. She wanted to be taken seriously, but she had noticed that a little charm could go a long way among these Spanish painters. Rebecca decided on a blue silk blouse and knee length black skirt with her black heels. For luck, she added her mother's pearl necklace that she wore when she needed a special boost. She caught herself in the bathroom mirror as she was turning off the lights for the evening. Was that really her? She hadn't noticed till now, but she looked different. Even almost three weeks here had changed her—her face had gained color, a few freckles, and her hair even seemed more at ease, sandy blonde curls fell effortlessly around her shoulders. She liked this brave-faced, worldly girl she saw in the mirror. Her Spanish too was improving—and Rebecca whispered to herself as the shopkeepers did, "*Qué guapa estás!* How pretty you are!" Never before and never since that moment had Rebecca felt so sure of herself.

With that confidence beneath her wings, Rebecca won the artists over handily. They were no match for her, really. Soto presented her proudly to the others and they welcomed her warmly with teasing cheers to repeat her whiskey toast. She could still see them, years later, with their sideburns and sport coats—their bellies just starting to reveal the success they were beginning to experience. They were an odd bunch—not entirely well matched: Soto was short but powerful and enigmatic with paintings that hung in the Koenig museum in Köln and the Museum of Modern Art in New York; Gonzalo Torres, whose massive iron shapes lived all over Spanish cities was rotund and liked to talk about anything and everything, especially busty women; German Rojas had founded the Abstract Art Museum with Zorita and Torres and was known for his geometric sculptures and paintings. Regalado, the rebel of them all, the untamed anarchist, his work was like Picasso's *Guernica* on a bad acid trip; and finally, Andrés Padilla wasn't a painter, but he wrote about them and traded the painters their art for his reviews and friendship. Rumor had it he was prone to depressive states. But Rebecca kept them talking—about their art, about American art, about Frida Kahlo and Diego Rivera. Her Spanish kept up and she smoothed over its rough edges with a finessed accent that made her sound less American, more like one of them.

"*Pero, no tienes ningún acento americano*" repeated Torres to Rebecca, then to Padilla, "*¿O qué?*, Andrés, she doesn't have any trace of American accent—it's unbelievable!"

"Well, maybe a little, Gonzalo. Besides, how many Americans have you met?"

"I hear them all the time on the television, you can't get away from them anymore since Franco died, they're on the television all the time!"

"Oh shut up about the television and Franco, Gonzalo! It's giving me indigestion!"

"What do you know, Andrés? You're nothing but an art critic…And everyone knows they know nothing about anything!" The painters roared with laughter at Andrés' expense.

They stayed like this, huddled in Santiago's bar, smoking and drinking till the early hours. Mostly Rebecca listened, but occasionally, she'd steer the conversation in a direction that would give her a better insight into their work. She wanted to know more about how things had changed since Franco died. It had only been three years since the dictator's death and Spain was still reeling from forty years under his reign.

"Tell me about when Franco died."

"*Madre mía*, what a question," said Regalado.

Andrés Padilla called out to Regalado, "Remember how we celebrated? What a relief when that motherfucker finally died."

They all looked around reflexively to see if anyone had heard them. Even with Franco gone and even at a bar like Jovi where they were among friends, it was still a risky thing for Andrés to say.

Regalado nodded in silence then began to speak slowly, as if recalling waking from a nightmare:

"*La madre que le parió*, I will never forget. I was in a taxi on my way to Madrid with Carmen. We had a friend who was a taxi driver. When he had to go to Madrid to buy a part for the car or something, he would let us ride with him—and we just paid for the fuel. This was before the Toledo Exhibition, so we went and bought all the copper materials for engraving, which were very heavy. Anyway, so he drops us off in Madrid and we went off to buy our materials and we went by the gallery. And he went to do his things. And we all met up at seven in the evening in a certain place with all our crap. Meanwhile, and this guy, he was *franquista*..."

This met with jeers from the band of artists gathered around Regalado, listening to his story.

"Yeah, one of those. And so Carmen and I are in the back of the car, and on the radio, all of a sudden they say there's an announcement, and then, what do you know, they announce the death of Franco. So because this guy's a Franco supporter, we don't say a thing. But I grabbed Carmen's hand and she grabbed mine, and we held hands as if to say, 'Yes!' And he didn't notice, but we, we held onto each others' hands like I don't think we'd ever held each other's hands. Like this." Regalado grabbed Andrés' hand and held it up for the bar to see. By now everyone was gathered around us. Regalado continued.

"We'd held hands of course before, but never like that, like on that day!"

The artists shouted in agreement, "Yes, yes, yes!"

Andrés then joined in. "You remember then how we went to Paris to see Soto? We went to Paris, about three days later. Me, you and Carmen—and we met Soto and Mercedes there."

Regalado nodded, then lowered his voice. "Yes, man, I needed to be with Communists! With Americans! Anyone but these fucking *falangistas*. That was a huge celebration. I have never in my entire life hugged anyone like that! It was like that for everyone, the day that son of a bitch died, eh? That son of a bitch who fucked up everyone's life..."

Torres turned to Rebecca and said, "You, you can't imagine what we've lived through. Living through a war, and the years after the war, and everything...And the dictatorship. Forty years. Forty years!

Regalado added almost whispering, "Hitler was in power, like, fewer than 10 years. Here, it was 40. And Hitler killed himself. This guy didn't just off himself and wave goodbye. This guy, what he wanted to do was go on hammering everyone's last nerve. Jesus, wouldn't it have been nice if Franco could have just killed himself. *Forty fucking years!*"

Rebecca listened intently to their stories. Each of them had been impacted by the war. She was beginning to understand their art; their paintings bore the scars.

Gonzalo turned to Rebecca, "And you must think after 40 years of Franco, we're in the middle ages in Spain."

"What are you saying? For me, I like it very much."

"Oh but we are backward, Rebecca, Cuenca is the most backward of all. Thank god we have Paris to escape to," said Andrés as they toasted another round of *copas*.

From then on, Rebecca was invited to all dinners they shared, treated to *copas*, and allowed to penetrate a world few women and no Americans had ever been allowed to enter. Rebecca could barely believe it herself.

She wrote her father and Zorita to share with them news of her progress:

> *"I feel indescribably at home here. I am not sure how it has happened, but I'm learning more than I could have ever imagined. Carmen says I must be part Spaniard. Do we have Spanish roots? Carmen swears we must."*

Chapter 15

As Rebecca got to know Soto's collective of painters, she also felt her bond with Carmen growing stronger. Shortly after the lunch with Soto, in addition to their weekly fish market outing, Carmen began inviting Rebecca over each week for Sunday lunch. Regalado was rarely home on Sundays, usually he headed out to Madrid or *el campo*, to the surrounding hills of Cuenca to hunt or sketch. Rebecca would be invited over just before 2pm, by which time most of the meal would have been prepared. Carmen left the final steps—the frying of the fish, the tossing of the tomatoes with the garlic, or the dressing of the salad—till Rebecca was there with her.

Carmen rarely let Rebecca help, but she would point to her almost-ready meal of *bacalao con salsa verde*, or Rebecca's favorite, *arroz con pollo*, and give Rebecca this or that tip. The girl would eagerly take notes in the little diary she kept as Flores detailed her work:

"Watch, see how I have cooked the chicken like this, in lots of oil, with lots of salt—on high I cooked it in the pan. Then you take it out, like so, and put it in a bowl aside and cover it with a plate. *Mira*, now I'm going to use the same pan and add more oil, it will look like a lot, but you need it, it makes the rice turn out so delicious. Eh, you see? So look, you add the oil, and then the chopped onions and let them sauté, till they're nice and soft. Then you add the green pepper and whatever else you want—artichoke hearts, asparagus tips, whatever you want. And you let that simmer, and then when it's all soft, really soft, you add the rice. Slowly. And just this much water, use your finger to measure it, here where the top of the finger is, that's where the water should be. Then you cover it, let it sit for a few minutes and add the chicken, cover it again. *¿Ves?*"

"Such a simple dish—we made it during the war to keep our stomachs full, it was always a dish for poor people. You could feed a whole house on a little rice and a quarter chicken. And we did! I made this many times for Regalado and me when we were broke, before Zorita had found Rego and started to sell his work. And even later, when he'd already had success, he hurt his back and we went months with hardly any money. I tell you, it was hard to put food on the table...though sometimes I think we were happiest then. It was just us, we'd left everything behind for each other and his work. . .Look, here, the rice is done now...you saw how I folded the chicken back in there? *Ven*, come see."

When the meal was ready, they would sit down to the table like old friends, Carmen still cloaked in her perfectly white apron, her *bata*, as she called it. The big window in the kitchen would be tied open and the view beheld the mountains around them. A fresh breeze would often blow across the table as they ate—sipping the champagne that Carmen would open on occasion. Maybe it was Carmen's divine culinary skills, maybe it was the champagne, but the two women, from opposite ends of the earth, with 35 years between them, were like school girls. They laughed about men, made fun of the artists, and slurped from their plates.

Carmen would recount stories from San Sebastián and Bilbao or exhibits she and Regalado had seen in Paris. Rebecca looked on with eager eyes, wishing she could remember these precious moments forever, for this was a life she had never lived before. But here she was, in this beautiful old woman's kitchen, speaking Spanish somehow, eating the most delicious food she'd ever eaten, as if this sort of thing happened to all 20-year-old Americans. And just when Rebecca could not imagine more pleasure from a Sunday lunch spent in this small town in Spain next to this modest wife of a master painter, Carmen would ask her, "*¿Te canto una canción de mi tierra*?" Shall I sing you a song from my earth? She meant of course her Basque homeland, but Rebecca loved the way Carmen said it, as if the song had come from the earth itself. And Rebecca would nod furiously, begging Carmen to sing. And then deep from Carmen's insides would emerge a sweet, sorrowful melody with words Rebecca could not understand. It sounded to Rebecca like a Japanese sailor, drunk on homemade hooch:

> *Triste bizi naiz eta hilko banintz hobe,*
> *badauzkat bihotzian, zenbait atsegabe.*
> *Maite bat maitatzen det, bainan haren jabe,*
> *sekulan izaiteko esperantzik gabe.*

When she was done, Carmen would translate the *Euskadi* words into Spanish for her, line by line*: I live sad and it'd be better if I died, I have so much grief in my heart. The one I love will never be mine, I have no hope of that.*

"Oh Carmen, it's so sad," Rebecca would say—for the songs were almost all very tragic.

And Carmen would laugh, "My dear, the Basques, we are a very serious people."

Carmen would sing slowly with her eyes closed and her hand grasping the green and white checked table cloth as the Basque sailor song overtook the two women in the kitchen, then all of Carmen's home, then the whole of Cuenca.

Regalado only joined Carmen and Rebecca for their Sunday afternoon lunch on one occasion. It was mid-July, Rebecca had been in Cuenca for nearly six weeks. The weather was increasingly hot and the nights were longer; white bed sheets hung from the windows and flapped in the light breeze. One Sunday, Carmen had made one of Rebecca's favorite meals—fried chicken breast and *tortilla española*—the Spanish equivalent of a potato omelet. As they were nearing the bottom of the champagne bottle that Carmen had begun to open religiously each Sunday ("*¿Por qué no*?" Carmen would say with a playful nudge at Rebecca), and about ready to slip into their respective *siestas*, the dogs began barking—signaling company.

"*Hombre*, who could that be?" Carmen said to Rebecca.

Seconds later, Regalado was standing in the kitchen doorway, looking wild and with a secret to tell. Rebecca started to excuse herself when Regalado explained the reason for his uncharacteristic Sunday afternoon appearance.

"*Mujer, rubia*—I have *pomelos*." A canvas bag hung from his forearm.

"*¿Pomelos?*" Rebecca was not familiar with the Spanish word.

"Like oranges, but bitter," Regalado explained.

"Ah, grapefruit!"

"Okay, *grape-fruit*, says the American!" agreed Regalado, repeating the word in English.

"*Bueno*," said Carmen, "We've had *pomelos* for three months now."

"Not these. These, *mi amor* are from *Aus-tral-ia,* he said, enunciating each syllable for effect."

"*Hombre*, what are you saying? Grapefruits from Australia? We have Javier's *huerta* right here and you're bringing grapefruits from Australia?

Regalado explained:

"Our friend, Miguel who drives taxi in Madrid, he has connections. Now that Franco's gone, I can't help but enjoy the delicacies coming in. It's my way of saying 'fuck you' to that bastard in the grave." Regalado looked up as if talking to the old *Caudillo* himself and said with a booming voice, "*Fuck you, Franco. I'm going to eat grapefruits from Australia.*

"*Bueno*, in that case, let's see them!" Carmen enjoined her unruly husband. "I have a bowl, I can put them out on the table."

"No—" replied Regalado wagging his finger at Carmen. "We will eat them immediately—do you still have room after your lunch of queens?"

"Of course!" Carmen dared him.

"*Venga*, let's go."

Regalado directed Carmen and Rebecca to join him at the marble counter where he handed them each a big pink grapefruit. Carmen drew a knife from the drawer to help cut the skin, and Rebecca stood dumbly, unsure of what to do next or how to react to Regalado. She'd barely gotten to know him; his presence made Rebecca uncomfortable.

"*¡Que no*!" shouted Regalado with gentle reprimand at Carmen. "*Vamos a hacerlo*, we are going to do it like wild beasts, *a la bestia*."

Regalado showed Rebecca and Carmen what he meant—he began tearing at the grapefruit, his long, dirty nails digging into the skin—breaking the thick rind apart, tearing away the inner skin and not at all paying attention to the delicacies of how the fruit had been formed. He just tore at it, till little pieces of it had flown everywhere and he was shouting nearly,

"*¡Así! ¡Así, Carmen*!" Carmen and Rebecca began to do the same, ripping and pulling at the grapefruits like wild women.

"*¡Eso es*!" He shouted, "Like savages! *¡Eso es*!"

Regalado was incorrigible, and his attack was unstoppable. They tore apart the grapefruits till their hands were bloodied with grapefruit juice, till the counter was covered in grapefruit rind and inner grapefruit skin. And then he commanded they try it—

"No bowls, plates or napkins, Carmen! Just eat it like so," and he placed a section of torn grapefruit into his mouth. Their hands were sticky and dripping with juice, and they laughed as they put little pieces of grapefruit meat in their mouths.

Carmen licked her lips in approval and Rebecca exclaimed, "This is the best grapefruit I've ever eaten! And I don't even like grapefruit!"

"All this effort and you don't even like grapefruit?!" Carmen doubled over laughing, then Regalado, and Rebecca followed, their mouths filled with more of the deliciously sweet, pink grapefruits. They ate every last piece, their hair and clothes messied from the operation. And when they were done, and Rebecca was about to excuse herself to her apartment, Carmen looked to Regalado and said:

"*Hombre*, this is why I love you. Look what happens when you bring home a couple of pieces of fruit. Just look what happens."

Chapter 16

BY THAT JULY when Rebecca stood with Carmen and Regalado in their kitchen, laughing over grapefruits, Rebecca's life in Cuenca had begun to take shape. She had her morning walks and her daily museum visits, she took *siestas* and talked with Carmen nearly every day, then visited with the painters in the afternoon. At nighttime she would socialize with the artists and their apprentices—in bars, restaurants and their homes. She took notes, she wrote, she danced around Carmen's flat and took it all in.

As the weeks wore on, Carmen had become like a mother and confidant to Rebecca. Carmen could tell when Rebecca was happy or sad, she saw it in the girl's eyes—from the bottom of the stairs, she said she could see it. Carmen taught her how to make *salsa verde*, how to de-salt the cod, how to heal an upset stomach. In Carmen's world olive oil, lemon and garlic could heal just about everything in the world—the flu, old age, and of course, hangovers. As the wife of a painter, Carmen had plenty of experience with that.

Cuenca was a town full of drunks. There were certainly as many drunks as there were artists, and as many artists as there were drunks. Some had what Carmen called *buena leche*—meaning when they drank too much, they became sweet and docile little lambs, men who you both pitied and loved for their expression of tears and affection. Then there were the other men, who had what Carmen called *mala leche*. Bad milk. Carmen had told Rebecca many times that Regalado fell into the latter category. His *borracheras* were legendary in town. In Spain, it was understood that in everyone's life, there are those times when nothing but booze will help. And Rego, the story went, whose father and brothers Franco's men slaughtered in the light of day by the bay of San Sebastián, who was estranged from his first wife and two daughters—who could blame the man for a little drunken binge?

In a town of drunks and a country that needed to do a little forgetting sometimes, there were a great many bars. These were not bars like Rebecca knew from home with neon signs and red vinyl booths. No, the bars in Cuenca were little rooms cut into buildings or the hillside, wherever you could fit a bar, a few bottles and a few *borrachos*. The bar men were big, stout things, who spoke in thick local dialect, but used words sparingly. They guarded over their bars like watchmen, and knew when to pour stiff. Most of them were generous with their pour. Tradition in Cuenca was to throw paper, tobacco, napkins on the floor. So by the end of the night, the floors were covered in a thick layer of trash. The bar men would sweep from closing till dawn, gathering the town's drunken leftovers into big piles. In the morning, their wives would pick up where they left off, shoveling the heaps into bags to be burned out back.

Although Rebecca was not yet 21, the legal drinking age in most parts of the United States, in Spain if you were tall enough to reach the bar, you were old enough to drink. Until that time, Rebecca's experience with alcohol had been limited to a glass of wine at dinner with her father or a beer at a college party. They must have seen it on her from afar; maybe it was her blonde curls that brought her so much attention in Cuenca, maybe that she looked like she needed spoiling. It was not hard to convince Rebecca—the bars were lovely, even the dingy ones.

There was *El Diablo*, a tiny bar off the main square. Two small windows behind the bar revealed the prickly Mediterranean hillside which sloped down to the *Júcar* river. The bar man was not particularly welcoming, but the late afternoon light kept clients coming back for afternoon drinks. Another bar below the Old Town in the new city served a little appetizer with each drink. While tapas were customary in Spain, the tapas at *El Anillo* were superior—cod stuffed peppers, fried egg and bacon served on hot toast, and the prized course that only came out after the sixth glass of wine, sizzling suckling lamb chops.

There were more bars buried beneath the rocks of the *Plaza Mayor* where married men went to find young women to sleep with. *Doña* Guadalupe's tavern behind the art museum had neither sign nor name. And mini stores like María de la Concepción's sold fresh bread, honey and *medio litro* beer cans, and let the drunks drink right there, right next to the register. María's daughter had a disability of some kind, so the two of them sat behind the counter with their thick glasses and flower aprons as the drunks made themselves at home and told them whatever story the beer conjured up next. But of all the bars, it was *Taberna Jovi* Rebecca loved the most. The bar men, Santiago and Ramón wore tuxedos. The walls were covered in dark wood paneling. And the seats were made of real leather. Santiago always welcomed Rebecca with open arms and a stiff martini. If you drank too much, a *tortilla* appeared magically at your table, made by Santiago's wife to dim the alcohol's effects.

Rebecca had also taken to Spain's late nights. She loved *La Calle*—the row of nightclubs that stayed open till dawn blasting American music. It helped push away the loneliness that had set in after a few weeks in Spain.

The week after Rebecca's grapefruit celebration with Carmen and Regalado she awoke in a fetal position in the *Jardín de Poetas* park without her shoes, the sun already high in the sky. Her head and ears pounded. She remembered the start of the previous night at Jovi with a few glasses of red wine, and then moving on to *El Anillo* with Torres' young apprentice, Francisco. She remembered they had made it to the grilled baby lamb chops tapas course, then moved on to a strange dance bar where the music was loud and Rebecca had started in on the vodka.

After that Rebecca could not remember how she got to the *Jardín de Poetas* or what had happened to her shoes. She would have to walk up the hill to the Old Town in her stocking feet, her dress stained and her hair a matted mess. She collected herself and navigated her way up the stone pathways to the old part of town. Rebecca hoped Carmen would be out with the dogs and would not again see her in such a state. But once she got going up the hill towards the *plaza*, Rebecca knew it was hopeless. The blonde American, shoeless and hung over and walking in the same clothes she'd been in the night before, would not go unnoticed. Carmen was not in sight, but Keiko, her Japanese artist friend yelled out in her ever-stilted Spanish,

"*¡Ey! Rebecca, ¿mucho borracho ayer o qué?*" Lots of drunk last night or what? Rebecca held up her hand to wave Keiko off, then ducked into the bar next to María's booze and honey shop. It was open but still empty at quarter after ten. Spaniards were a late-rising bunch, thank god.

Rebecca ordered a *café con leche* and some toast. Unfortunately, the barkeeper must have had his own *borrachera* the previous night, because his moves were painfully slow. She curled up at the end of the bar, trying to make herself invisible, trying to stay still enough to keep the nausea at bay. An old man sat in front of the slot machine, popping in *peseta* after *peseta*. He or another man like him always occupied the stool there, feeding coins to the machine endlessly. Rebecca had her head resting on the bar, her arms curled around it when she heard a familiar voice call out to the barkeeper:

"Antonio! I need a beer! And get one for the pretty lady in the corner too!"

Shit. Shit, shit, Regalado, thought Rebecca.

Regalado approached the counter, leaving a wide birth around Rebecca.

"*Muy buenas, americana.* Carmen sent this."

Rebecca raised her head up and Regalado handed her a still warm hard-boiled egg.

"Helps with the hangover."

"How did Carmen know I am hung-over?"

"*Rubia*, do you think that woman misses much? She got worried when you didn't come home last night, then waited at the window. She saw you marching miserably up the hill and sent me to find you. But, you know, nothing helps a hangover so much as a little more alcohol. Hair of the dog you Americans call it."

"*No, por favor*, I'll throw up." The room was spinning now, and the fact that Carmen had seen her was making the nausea worse.

"Antonio, forget the beer, get her a Bloody Mary. *Guapa*, have trust in me, this and the egg and you'll feel better soon."

Rebecca obeyed Regalado meekly. Sure enough, Regalado's remedy worked, in a few minutes she started feeling better. Rebecca sat up a little, trying to pull herself together and get back home. Regalado looked at her and laughed.

"You know, all artists are drunks," Regalado informed her.

"I am no artist," Rebecca replied, "I just study them."

"Well then, call it research."

Regalado stayed with Rebecca until he was sure she was well enough to walk the rest of the way home to her apartment, then bid her goodbye. Rebecca could see why Carmen loved him—beneath the rough exterior he was softer than Rebecca had imagined. There was a kind of sweetness to him that she had not expected.

"*Bueno, nos vemos*, see you around," said Regalado as he patted the bar top and moved to leave.

"Thank you, Rego—for this morning."

"It's nothing—go sleep, you'll feel better when you wake."

Rebecca did sleep—for the rest of the day, till Carmen came knocking with a bowl of fish stew. She looked Rebecca up and down as if to make sure Rebecca was all there, her limbs still attached. But she said nothing about the *borrachera* or that she'd sent Rego to find her. She just told Rebecca "Eat this, you need the protein. I am going to walk the dogs."

After Carmen had gone, Rebecca sat in bed eating stew, thinking about that morning with Regalado. What was it, what had it been about him that she couldn't shake from her mind?

Chapter 17

Rebecca regretted her *borrachera* but fortunately didn't have much time to dwell on it. She was preoccupied with an exposition that she was helping with at the *Museo de Arte Abstracto*. The museum had just undergone a large extension that had tripled the size of the space and was now attracting interest from across the globe. Torres had brought an artist friend from Germany to exhibit and there was much work to be done. Rebecca helped unwrap dozens of canvases and sculptures, and worked closely with the museum's art director to prepare the exhibition room and printed materials. Her days were spent at the museum and her nights were spent along the back steps of the *Plaza Mayor* with the hordes of other teenagers and college students who were home for the summer. Soto was in Paris again, and she would not meet with Zorita until August. There was nothing but art and *cerveza* for as far as Rebecca could see—and she was having the time of her life.

On the weekends Rebecca would head to the *Playa Municipal* with Soto's daughters. It wasn't a real beach, of course—Cuenca was 200 miles from the nearest beach in Valencia. But at the base of the mountain, with the town hanging hundreds of feet above, a small dam had been created and the edge of the river lined with barrels of sand brought in from the south. The water was a bright pale green from the minerals in the river. It was freezing cold, too—but no one cared, especially in the heat of the midday Spanish sun. Old ladies sunbathed, teenagers floated down the river in rafts, and a restaurant served cold beer and warm *tortilla española.*

Rebecca thought often about what it would be like to just finish college and set up a life in Cuenca. It was a place like none other she had known before. She loved its secrets, its hanging hams, its dingy bars, low-lying rivers, and expansive mountainsides. She had not stopped her morning walks, either—these she kept to religiously. It was her time to take in all that she was experiencing, all that was speeding by without slowing down enough to hold onto a little longer.

And so, despite Rebecca's curiosity about Regalado and their interaction several days before following her *borrachera*, she didn't think much about him. Then one morning, Rebecca was returning from her morning walk. She had walked past *San Isidro* cemetery and was winding her way around the mountain highway, back to the main road that led to the *Plaza Mayor.* The town was still quiet, as it always was till late morning. Rebecca had collected some fresh rosemary for Carmen on her walk and was absorbed in her thoughts when she walked right into Regalado.

"Ay, Rebecca—*¡Muy buenas!*" said Regalado. From the look of it, he'd been up all night, his hair was messy and he'd not shaven for a few days. But he had that wild look in his eye that she'd seen in Carmen's kitchen, and then at the bar the morning after her binge.

"Very good day," replied Rebecca as she'd learned was the customary greeting in Cuenca.

"It's my turn today for the *borrachera,*" Regalado confessed.

"Ah, you should have one of Carmen's eggs," said Rebecca.

"It's true, it's true...I was thinking of having a coffee and a beer first though. Will you join me?"

"*Claro que sí*," replied Rebecca. She was eager to spend some time with Regalado...he was the one artist she'd had the hardest time convincing to work with her.

"This way, I like Bar Mangana."

Regalado led the way up the hill to the highest point of the old town. Rebecca had been there a couple of times—she liked how isolated it was from the hum of the *Plaza Mayor*, and they had a nice, covered patio. Rebecca walked awkwardly next to Regalado. He seemed very tall to her, and a little less comfortable in his skin than she'd seen him before.

"How's the art going?" Rebecca asked, trying to sound casual.

"Ooph, it's a fucking pain in the ass. You gonna make me talk about art all morning after this hell of a *borrachera*?"

"If you'd prefer we can talk about the *borrachera*," said Rebecca.

"*Vale*, you have a point there—can't remember a damn thing from that. But you know, I hate talking about art. Talking about art is like talking about sex. Why talk about it when you can just do it? You just have to fuck, it's a waste of time to discuss it...I'm sorry, I'm sorry—I'm such an ass—you're an art historian. That's what you do with your goddamn life and here I am shitting all over it."

"It's okay, Rego—you're right, it's much more fun to make art than talk about it. I won't take it the wrong way," said Rebecca.

"Alright, you're kind to forgive me there. So tell me, Rebecca, Rebecca—what do you think of Cuenca? Of Spain? Like you thought it would be?"

"I didn't have any idea what it would be like. It feels like Mars might feel—entirely different than anything I've ever experienced. America is not like Spain. New York is not like Cuenca."

Regalado replied:

"Spain is a bunch of retards. Not the Basques—they're something else. But most of Spain, I am telling you...*Vaya*, there I go again shitting on everything. I can't help it sometimes, you know? There really are so many assholes in this world...Franco, all the generals who ran around in their little uniforms, all these people who think Spain is free now that Franco is gone—they're a bunch of idiots. Nothing will change here, nothing. But you Americans, you're not any better—we're all idiots. The Spanish, the Italians, the Germans, the South Americans, the Arabs. All assholes, all of us. Except the Basques, the Basques, now there's a people."

Regalado chain smoked as they waited on their coffee. He was not polished like the other painters. But to Rebecca, he seemed to be the smartest one of the bunch. She knew from studying his work at the Museum that Regalado was experimenting with techniques that none of the other painters were working with. Like his hair and that look in his eyes, his paintings were riskier—they were full of rage, his paintings, the canvas overtaken by something almost other-worldly. Regalado did not listen to rules or reason in his painting, and he hadn't been trained classically, so he was not slowed by the limitations of technique or schooling. Rebecca was not surprised that he talked as gruffly as he painted. Bursts of color and fury flying everywhere. Then he would catch himself, and pull back, aware that he was not alone.

"You, tell me about you, Rebecca," Regalado said, lighting another cigarette from the one hanging out of his mouth.

"What do you want to know? I am much less interesting than art or *borracheras*," Rebecca said, cocking her head with a self-deprecating smile.

"What do you find interesting about a bunch of middle age artists in some lost corner in Spain? You can't really believe that crap Zorita says about lifting all of Spain up in the eyes of the world through our art. Tell me you don't believe that."

Regalado's honesty was refreshing to Rebecca. It wasn't that the others hadn't been open or honest with her, but he really cut through the garbage. Rebecca laughed and smiled at Regalado.

"Zorita's an idealist, there is no doubt—"

Regalado cut in "—And it's easy to have that much faith when you've got that much fucking money. *Hombre*."

"Yes, that helps!" agreed Rebecca. "But the work is different, and the climate here—I mean now that Franco's gone and things are changing—or could change anyway, it's creating interesting things. I don't know, I don't think I'll be able to necessarily achieve what Zorita hopes once I go back home—not because I won't want to, but, how do you say, it might be a little unrealistic, yes?"

"Ah ha! I was right."

"But wait, wait, the art IS very different from what's going on elsewhere. It has its own rhythm, its own complexities. I like it very much—and that's the point, I wouldn't be here if I wasn't moved by it."

Regalado looked at Rebecca pensively, then said, "You're okay, Rebecca. You're okay. Don't let my cynical ass fuck that up."

They finished their coffees, Regalado his beer, and then suddenly, leaving *pesetas* on the table to pay, Regalado was up and gone.

"The studio calls—you'll excuse me."

Rebecca watched him walk down the hill to his studio, his gait a little taller and quicker than when she'd met him an hour earlier. She wanted to know more about him—behind the rough exterior she felt something very gentle about him. She didn't know when they'd meet again, but she hoped it would be soon. She had enjoyed her breakfast with a hung-over Regalado more than she'd enjoyed a half dozen more formal meetings with Rojas or Torres.

Rebecca headed down the hill, passing Regalado's studio as she went; she could hear Flamenco music playing from inside. She smiled to herself as she thought of him, shaking off his hangover and cursing the world—why were the most interesting ones always the most destructive?

She returned to her apartment to find that Carmen had already made her bed and left a clean towel. A fresh pound cake was cooling on the marble counter. The painters who had once stayed at the apartment where Rebecca was now living spoke of Carmen's legendary homemaking skills, envious of Regalado. Carmen did not simply make the bed. She washed the embroidered sheets every three days. She ironed the linens by hand after they'd hung out to dry for a day. She folded the sheets in perfect grid form which allowed her later to make the bed perfectly symmetrical. She tucked in the corners, pulled at the sheets till they were straight and perfect, going around the bed 10 times just to make sure the sheets were folded exactly right and adhering to her grid—or her *pautas* as she called them. She folded the sheet over and under the top duvet, fluffed each pillow and then pulled and tucked some more. Now that was a bed you could sleep in. Carmen considered it a personal philosophy of hers that every human being on the planet should have a clean bed to sleep in...and know how to make their own bed.

But no one could compete with Carmen's ironing skills. The first time Carmen had ironed one of Rebecca's blouses, she left it hanging from the door of the antique dresser. It looked like an art piece, perfectly white and crisp, not a single wrinkle.

Vaya mujer, thought Rebecca.

Chapter 18

Bullfighting season was in full force in Spain. The *Feria de Julio* had come to Valencia and since she'd missed San Fermín in July, Rebecca was determined to attend at least one bullfight in Spain. Carmen agreed Rebecca needed to go:

"You have to go...It is a gruesome custom in Spain, but a beautiful one. And you know, the *toreros*, the bull fighters, don't think they haven't much respect for the bulls. The bulls are very smart, and the *toreros* they know this. The *toreros*, they learn to stand right where the bull can't see them, because the bulls, they can see on all sides except right in front of them." Carmen gestured with her fingers where the bull's horns would be and moved her head back and forth to illustrate.

"See, they can't see here, right in front of them. That's how the *torero* gets them, they stand right there. But they have to get close enough or they'll be in the bull's line of vision...You know, Rego was a *torero*.

"No way!"

"*Sí, sí, sí.* He wanted to be a bullfighter. And he was always with bullfighters. He would tell them, 'All bull fighters want to be painters and I want to be *torero*. Let's switch places.' *Sevilla* was full of boys like him, all lining up to learn to dance with a bull. After they killed his father—the fascists—it made him unafraid. So he went to *Sevilla.* Regalado would make seven *pesetas* a week as an apprentice bullfighter. He sent home two *pesetas* to his mother who had gone back to her home in San Sebastián, paid his rent with another two, and had the remaining three *pesetas* to eat and entertain himself. He ran around with a rough crowd there but he'd sell his drawings on the street for a coin or two, whatever anyone would give him. He was a *torero* for seven years. Until one day, at a huge festival in Granada, Regalado was fighting a particularly fierce bull and the bull got him. It pinned him to the ground and stuck its horn in his left thigh. It pierced him all the way through, out through his ass."

"No way, he was gored by a bull?" Rebecca asked, incredulous.

"Yes, the doctor said had it been a centimeter this way or that, he would have died from the puncture. Regalado wanted to go back into the ring, but he couldn't run as fast anymore and had lost a little confidence. His mother and friends convinced him to leave bullfighting and return to San Sebastián to find work as an artist. He didn't want to go, but there was nothing more for him in *Sevilla* without the bulls and he needed time to heal. If he had never been a *torero,* I don't know if Regalado would have become a painter. Sometimes one thing leads to another, *¿sabes?*

Anyway, *niña*...It's an enormous spectacle...*A mí,* it makes me sad, I cannot help it. But it is also very beautiful, and the bulls, and the *toreros,* they are very brave to do what they do."

Carmen made a few calls and discovered that Torres' apprentice, Francisco, would be going to Valencia and he was happy to take

Rebecca along. Rebecca piled into a big van filled with Francisco's friends and their girlfriends that Saturday morning. They sang Spanish folk songs all the way there, as the van made its way through the mountainside towns to Valencia. During her stay, Rebecca had not left Cuenca and was eager to see another part of the country. She watched as the landscape changed from Cuenca's limestone hills and pine forests to flat red countryside. The air began to change till Rebecca thought she could nearly smell the sea 50 miles ahead of them. Valencia's Old Town was different, too—it was bigger than Cuenca, with large stone bridges that criss-crossed its perimeter.

Francisco navigated their van through the one-way streets and past the *Plaza de la Virgen* and cathedral to the other side of town. Rebecca watched the scenes unfolding outside the window while the others chatted away in Spanish. Gypsies had their fold-up carts and their wares, old women sold sodas by the side of the road, and teenagers walked in excited groups towards the arena.

The group descended on the *plaza de toros* like triumphant teenagers. They were there to witness the ultimate Spanish art— beloved, hated, but an art nonetheless. Rebecca bought *Fanta de limón* from an old gypsy in the parking lot, then made her way with the group inside the *plaza de toros*. The exterior hung like a proud Arab mosaic—left over from another time when the Moors still ruled. But this was not the custom of Arabs. This was pure Spain. And here Rebecca had come to watch this mortal dance. They bought the cheapest seats, which meant the sun would be in their faces till it dipped below the upper level of the arena. They brought floppy hats and umbrellas to soften its harsh Spanish effects. Rebecca could hear old men around them telling stories in deep, raspy voices—about *toreros* they'd seen, about legendary studs. A man wet the reddish ground in the bullring, readying for the spectacle that was about to begin. Francisco explained to Rebecca the rules of the bullfight.

"The bulls are down there, in that pen. See that one there, trying to get out—he knows he's in for a fight." Rebecca could see a big black bull ramming the gate just beneath a row of seats below them.

"Is he angry?"

"Well, he's not happy, he's been penned up like that...and see that ribbon, pinned to his neck? It's called a *divisa*; it shows the bloodline and gets them riled up."

As the trumpet sounded and the gates could be heard releasing, the crowd erupted into cheers. Rebecca's heart raced and she sat forward on the cement amphitheater bench—below her entered three *toreros*, one after the other. Their costumes were of blues and greens and blacks, with pink socks neatly pulled up to their knees, emerging from what looked like ballet slippers. They made their way around the ring, men on horses following them. Once they completed their first circle, two of the *toreros* exited the ring and stood behind a large barrier where they watched, heads peeking over the wooden barrier too narrow for bulls to enter.

"*Señoras y Señores*!" shouted the master of ceremonies. "For our first round, we have Spain's beloved *torero*, Juan Frontera!"

The crowd screamed and flowers flew from the sky into the ring. A small looking man emerged from the sidelines and the crowd screamed again—he wore tight black pants with yellow tights and donned a black cap. He bowed and more flowers flew at him.

Rebecca sat at the edge of her seat, eager and afraid for the bull to emerge. Then with a loud bang, it did. It was enormous, and it trotted out of the pen at full speed. The *torero* stood firmly in the center of the ring, letting the bull take him in. Rebecca saw what Carmen meant about having respect for the bull. The bull began to trot around and the *torero* pulled out his pink cape. The bull then readied himself and aimed his horns for the *torero*, kicking up his leg once and then barreling full steam ahead for Juan Frontera. But by the time the bull reached his target, Juan Frontera had side-stepped the animal's field of vision and the bull could not find him.

Rebecca loved each minute of it. She barely spoke to Francisco and his friends—she was completely taken by the spectacle. Yes, Carmen had been right—it was the greatest spectacle she'd ever seen. Football didn't come close.

The second *torero* to enter the ring was Roberto Blanco. He was young but known for his extreme bravery. Rebecca watched him, wide-eyed as he sank to his knees in front of the door where, moments later, a bull would emerge.

"*¿Qué hace?*" Rebecca asked Francisco, worried.

"It's called *rodillas.* He will wait for the bull on his knees," Francisco explained.

Rebecca gulped in waves of hot air as Blanco raised up his cape, his head up, defiant, only his legs behind him revealing his fear; he crossed himself and the door flew open. And there came a massive bull straight for Blanco. Still on his knees, Blanco maneuvered his cape expertly and the bull ran past him. Then Blanco leapt to his feet and the crowd cheered wildly. Rebecca exhaled.

"Holy shit."

For the first few minutes of his fight, Blanco fought beautifully. But then it came time for the killing. Blanco could not kill the beast with a clean thrust. Too young, too inexperienced, too afraid—whatever it was, the crowd turned silent as Blanco and two other *toreros* together tried and failed to kill the bull. An old *picador* was forced to come out and slay the beast himself. By the end, no one clapped and Blanco left the ring, bloodied and shamed.

"*¡Qué disgusto!*" shouted Francisco as Blanco retreated.

The other *toreros* took their turns but the mood of the crowd had changed and when Blanco returned to the arena, there were no cheers; the excitement his *rodillas* stunt had created was gone. Blood still covered his suit—there would be no costume change. The crowd collectively shared a bad taste on their tongues. Secretly, Rebecca wondered if he would not deserve a horn. Not in the head or neck, but maybe the arm—to teach him a lesson. But this next bull, white sand colored—not black like the others—was a lovely thing. All the bulls were impressive to Rebecca but this bull was different. It seemed intelligent, graceful, noble. After Blanco and the bull engaged in a brief dance, suddenly the crowd began to chant wildly.

Francisco pointed up at a balcony, high up in the stands where a man waved a white flag. The crowd erupted into cheers.

"What's happening?" Rebecca asked Francisco.

"The *presidente* of the fight, he has just announced that the bull should live!"

Behind Rebecca, she heard an old *abuelo* exclaim in raspy *castellano*, "Forget this young know-nothing *torero*, what a beauty of a beast this bull! What a day, Valencia. What a beautiful day."

Roberto Blanco left the ring dejected, but the crowd went wild for the bull whose life had been spared.

After the bullfight, all of them walked to the beach to swim in the ocean before heading home. The sea was calm and green—like the river in Cuenca. The others stripped down and threw themselves into the water. Rebecca stood pensively at the shore, her skirt gathered in her hands.

The bullfight made her think of Cuenca's artists, especially Regalado. She understood now why Regalado might have been a good *torero.* He was as wild as the bulls—and like them, he did not care if he would live or die, he just wanted to dance with fate, whatever the result. Rebecca wondered if she had it in herself to be as bold as those *toreros.*

Could she look a bull in the eye and be ready to die for the art? Would she have the will to survive a horn through her thigh? That was what these bullfighters and artists did each day—especially when Franco had been in power. That was what drew Rebecca to what they were doing. It was the context they had evolved in, that their painting looked an oppressive authority in the face and responded, *still we will paint. Still we will dance. Still we will be free.* Regalado would laugh at Rebecca's conclusions. "They are just bulls I paint!" he'd say. "What in the hell does it have to do with the fascists?" But the bulls were subversive, thought Rebecca—they were bold, and unafraid. The bulls were full of heat, their balls hanging from their backside. Yes, if she had the chance, if she could make good on her promise to Zorita, this is what Rebecca would tell the world about *El Grupo* from Cuenca.

Chapter 19

REBECCA DID NOT meet the painters again till a week later, when a *borrachera* began at Soto's. Soto had returned home from Paris eager to gather *El Grupo*. He told Carmen to pass along the invitation. Carmen made a rule of never going to the painters' *tertulias*—they were not for her, she said firmly. "I am not an artist, I don't understand their world. I don't want any of it." But Rebecca loved these gatherings the most. She was fawned over and doted upon, and she could not resist the attention from this team of creators. Their energy for art and life was infectious—and Rebecca loved them all the more when the whiskey started tugging at their tongues.

That night Carmen left Rebecca *arroz con pollo* in a small sauce pan on the stove. She could already hear the teenagers gathering in the *plazas* below, their hormones echoing against the hills and reverberating back to the beer bottles they carried in their hands. She loved what they loved about these summer nights—they were hot, long and free. Franco had died and the country was coming out of a 40-year stupor. She loved how far her home in New York was, how different this life was, just a few thousand miles away. A few thousand miles! This was another universe. And the freedom she felt here made her giddy.

Rebecca sat at the table in the middle of her apartment, eating her *arroz con pollo*, slowly relishing her favorite of all of Carmen's dishes. Carmen managed to cook it perfectly each time —tender rice cooked softly in olive oil, let to simmer with onions, peppers and artichoke hearts, then cooked with tender chunks of chicken thigh meat. She could hear Carmen rattling off the recipe as she ate. Rebecca devoured the very last grain of rice, then slipped on her shoes, out the door, giving a knock at Carmen's door as she left so Carmen knew she was leaving and, as Carmen insisted upon, could prepare the girl's bed.

Rebecca hurried down the stairs, anxious to be there, excited to see Soto, Rojas, Torres, and of course, Regalado. Their wives had long tired of the philosophical talk of art and existence that grew increasingly meaningful in direct proportion to how much alcohol they'd drunk. But she was young yet, and eager to be among men who praised her and listened to her. She wanted to be among them again. They smelled like oil paints and cigarettes and she found it addictive. She never thought for a moment as she walked up the hill through the old city where she'd end up that night. No one told her one minute you could be eating *arroz con pollo*...and the next minute conceiving a baby by another woman's man in a dank art studio at dawn.

No one told her that's how life can turn, and some things you don't get to take back.

Chapter 20

Soto's apartment was where all his late night exploits took place. The studio was sacred—it was for painting, not for hordes of drunken artists. But the home he shared with his wife, Mercedes, was fair game. Looking over the *Plaza Mayor* on one side and the canyon on the other (it, too, was located on what Carmen called the "fascist side" of the mountain), it was well situated to be the central meeting ground for dinners and salons. It was an apartment typical of the *Casco Antiguo*—low-hanging ceilings, exposed wood beams, tiny kitchens and bathrooms (when the buildings were built in the 16th century, there was no running water, no washing machines or great bathtubs). A long, jumbled stairwell led three stories up to Soto's flat. The ceilings were crooked too, which gave it an Alice in Wonderland feel. When you came in, there was a tiny sitting room where the family usually had breakfast, but rounding the corner, there was a large living room with an enormous picture window looking out over the hills. Throughout the summer, students partied till dawn on the steps below the apartment.

Rebecca stopped at Jovi for a quick drink to brush off the nerves that always started before she met with *El Grupo*. She also wanted to say hello to Santiago, of whom she'd grown quite fond. Then, she headed to Soto's. It was well after 11 p.m. —about the time Saturday nights got going in Spain. She had made sure to nap after lunch so she'd be alert and able to stay awake throughout the night.

When Rebecca got to Soto's, Torres and Rojas were there, already arguing about something, their usual banter. Soto welcomed her at the door with a kiss on each cheek and planted a neat whiskey in her hand.

"To never having my paintings hang over a couch, and to you, making us all *famosos*!"

"*¿Famosos*?" questioned Molina. "Fame doesn't matter to me, I just want enough *pesetas* to buy some *jamón ibérico de vez en cuando.* Those ones they feed with acorns."

"To *jamón de bellota*!" Rebecca raised her glass and the painters cheered at their favorite Spanish delicacy.

"Come," said Soto to her, "join us in the *salón*, you must weigh in on the Dalí versus Magritte debate. They are both idiots, if you ask me."

Rebecca laughed at Soto's description of two of Spain's finest artists as idiots. It was hardly the case, but it was funny to hear Soto's dismissal of them. She entered the living room and greeted the other two painters. Rojas was in his formal suit, while Torres had on his usual faded sport coat with black pants. He tried to hide his belly, but the man liked beer and it showed.

"*¿Que tal*, Rebecca? *Qué guapa estás*," said Torres.

Rojas added, "She always is lovely, aren't you Rebecca? You put us old pigs to shame."

"*No, ¿que dices?*, what are you saying," said Rebecca to Rojas, "You are still a young pig!"

"*No se hizo la miel para la boca del asno*," Rebecca heard Torres say. She couldn't be sure entirely what he meant by the idiom, but she gathered it had something to do with putting honey in the mouth of a donkey.

"You're right, Torres. I *am* old and crotchety and deserve to be fed hay by fat old ladies. While you, *rubia*, are as graceful as a swan," said Rojas.

Rebecca pulled up a chair to join Rojas and Torres. Candlelight danced about the apartment, illuminating the white walls against the old wood beams. Mercedes had set the wooden table in the living room with a white linen. Candlesticks burned, their wax melting down the sides of bottles of wine. She'd prepared plates of *tortilla española, mortadela* and *queso manchego.*

"Where is Mercedes?" called out Rebecca to Soto, who was working on the music selection.

"You know Mercedes, she's like Carmen, no parties for her! She went to her sister's place in the new town, you know, she can't put up with the whiskey. Or me with the whiskey. I try to tell her it helps with the painting, but she won't have any of it."

Torres agreed, "Yes, María will come if it's for an art opening or the magazines are there—let me tell you, she comes when the magazines are there! But otherwise, forget it! A married man, and I have to lead a bachelor's life to have any fun!"

Rojas, whose wife came with him nearly everywhere said, "I don't know what is wrong with your wives, but mine is very easy."

"Then why is she not here tonight?" said Torres.

"Well, sometimes it does do a man good to have some whiskey."

"Ah hah! You see? We get married, only to have to drink alone," said Soto.

"You'll see, Rebecca, you'll see—are you going to do that to your man one day?" asked Torres.

"Only if he turns into an ass, like you all!" Rebecca teased, the three painters cheering in return. They went on like this till midnight when more painters from their *pandilla* joined them. Andrés Padilla showed up, then Toset. Rebecca wondered if Regalado would come. She had hoped to see him most.

"Is Regalado coming tonight?" Rebecca asked Soto, trying not to sound too invested.

"*Bueno*, you know Rego—that man runs to another beat. He's probably in *barrio* San Antón with two women and a bottle of whiskey. Who knows with that one!"

Just as Soto had said it, Regalado made his appearance. The door swung open and Regalado flung his arms into the air with a whoop. As usual, when he actually showed up, Regalado was the life of the party. He made his way around the room, hugging the painters or tugging on their ear as a hello. Rebecca watched him from the corner of the living room and unconsciously moved behind the table into the shadows. She liked Regalado but something about him made her both excited and nervous. He was like the bulls she'd seen at the bullfight in Valencia—you could never tell what he would do next.

"Soto," yelled Regalado across the room, "*¡Un brindis!*" The others turned to listen to Regalado's toast. Rebecca watched from the corner, she'd still not said hello to Regalado, but she was sure he had seen her.

"You know, we have been very fortunate us painters this summer. For Zorita, in his infinite desire to see Spanish abstract art take over the world, has brought us a gift. Now, Zorita is in Italy with his marble busts that he loves so much, so I cannot thank him personally. But, I can thank the girl he brought, and who I know, has spent her summer taking many notes and doing much research on us—*Us*! Who would have thought anyone would give a shit about us! To Rebecca!"

The other painters raised their glasses in agreement in Rebecca's direction. She inhaled, taking them all in, Soto there with his hair pulled over his balding head, Torres with his belly and moustache, Rojas, frail as ever, but always the most poised of the bunch, then Regalado, legs splayed and towering over the others. Regalado's eyes were trained on her. Rebecca raised a glass in return.

"*Muchas gracias*, Regalado, Soto, everyone. The honor is all mine."

It was a stunning night—debates were had, plans were made, exhibits were drawn up. The painters danced with one another to the music—it had begun with Miles Davis but by two in the morning, they'd given themselves over to Spanish pop melodies with songs like *Vivir Así es Morir de Amor.* Soto kept the whiskey coming, and let the music play loud. Rebecca was stirred by the alcohol, the company, and Regalado's toast. She thought to herself, *In all my life, I'll never forget this; I'll never forget they let me in.*

Just then Regalado put a 45 on Soto's record player. Rebecca heard the scratchy prelude, then the sound of a guitar, hands clapping and a man's voice; pained, melancholy, unusually high. Flamenco. Regalado began to clap his hands together with the music, his arms extended over his head, the right hand cupped tightly and the fingertips of that hand slapping his left palm. The others made room for Regalado to enter the center of the room as they stood from Soto's couches and armchairs to surround him. The man's voice trembled through the speakers, "*No puedo contenerme cuando te veo, tu mirada me sigue, tus ojos me siguen, no puedo contenerme.*"

Regalado clapped, his head turned to the side, his long straight nose, black eyes and strong chin turned downward, his breath following the music's rhythm; Soto threw out an "*¡Olé!*" Regalado turned in a tight circle as if a flamenco dancer, his feet stomping the floor with the same staccato beat of the guitar. Slowly he made his way around the room, dancing before each painter till he made his way to Rebecca. Regalado stood in front of her, his eyes now fixed on hers, unmoving, unwilling to look away. Regalado reached out for Rebecca, his arm encircling her back, pulling her towards the middle of the circle.

"*¡Olé!*" Shouted Soto again, encouraging Rebecca to dance.

Regalado positioned Rebecca's arm over her head to mirror his stance, then he motioned to her to step slowly around him in a circle. His eyes did not leave hers. She could not tell what lay behind his black eyes, but her entire body felt like a flaming cup. She could not contain how Regalado made her feel…she didn't want to. She just wanted to dance like this, the sound of the guitar, the light of the candles, the look in Regalado's eyes carrying her into a world she'd never visited before. *Tac, Tac, Tac* went their hands, clapping in unison, *Tac, Tac,* the gypsy record filling the room with the strangest, most beautiful music Rebecca had ever heard.

They danced like this till the record ran out. Regalado and Rebecca, then each of the painters took their turn dancing in the middle of the room, like young men with no fear. They clapped and whooped and hollered *¡Olé!* Till they had exhausted themselves and decided it was time to celebrate with a beer on the town. Rebecca's heart was still pounding from the wild, unflinching look she'd seen in Regalado's eyes as they danced.

The men of *El Grupo* and Rebecca emerged from Soto's to walk up the hill to *Doña* Guadalupe's bar. She was always open till nearly dawn and the cocktails were cheap. Most of the painters stood by the bar, again likely arguing over whether Dalí had been the best surrealist or if he was just a phony. Rebecca sat at a table with Regalado and Torres. Torres rattled on about his deal with the city to install a large sculpture in one of the central *plazas*. Rebecca noticed Regalado had grown quiet, and she wished Torres would leave them to talk alone. Rojas eventually called Torres over to the bar; Regalado and Rebecca were grateful for a few minutes without him.

Now that she had him to herself, she didn't know what to say. They sat quietly for a few moments, which felt like an eternity to Rebecca. As much as she wanted to start talking to break the heavy silence between them, she sensed she needed to wait for his cue. And then it came. Regalado leaned in and growled gently in her ear, "*Vente conmigo*." Come home with me.

Rebecca studied his face and tried to pretend he hadn't meant it. But his eyes were unflinching; he stared at her, the cigarette between his fingers burning, the ash at the end growing. He was waiting for her to answer what he seemed to consider a fair question.

"*¿Es broma*?" She asked, sounding younger than she meant to.

"I'm not joking. Come with me," he repeated his entreaty.

She realized he was an adult and this was a conversation not with a teenage boy but with a real life man who somehow, she'd caught the attention of. A man who was now calling her bluff. Rebecca excused herself from Regalado to step outside. She was sweating, between her legs she felt a pulsing sensation. "*Vente conmigo*." His words ran through her, quickening her heartbeat and sending shivers up her spine. She walked back and forth nervously in the stone alleyway outside Jovi. *This can't go anywhere*, she told herself. *It's wrong, this is Carmen's man, and it needs to stop.* But her internal dialogue was no match for how she felt from her mouth to her sex. Up and down inside her flowed *That Feeling*, and it felt too good to say no.

Regalado emerged from the bar, raised his eyebrows as if to say, "*I'm not going to ask twice. Are you in, or not?*" and kept walking. She turned and followed behind him.

Chapter 21

Regalado led Rebecca up the hill to his studio. They did not speak as they walked. They were both tipsy and she was shivering from the July night that had turned cold. At the door to the squat apartment building where his studio was located, Regalado gestured to the second story windows and pulled the key from his pocket. They passed into a dark entryway and Regalado started up the stairs. He walked with heavy steps ahead of her, turning to wait for her at the top of the landing outside the door to his studio.

When she reached him, Regalado wrapped his arms around her tiny waist. She looked into his eyes, hoping to catch a glimpse of understanding in him. What was it there? In those black planets looking back at her? Or were they too eager? *Salvaje.* She could feel his hands moving across her body, at the hips, up and down her back. It felt good. He was warm and tasted like whiskey and coffee. He tasted like a man—or what she had always imagined a fully grown man would taste like. Rebecca could feel every piece of her body pulsing in anticipation as he kissed her there in the stairwell.

"*Venga,*" he growled into her ear, "*Vamos.*" She nodded without a word.

Chapter 22

There was nothing that night outside that bus and her two eyes. And of course, the fire, now dimmed, but still burning at her intestines. *Be still. Be still.* Rebecca whispered to the surrounding black as if the words might hit the glass window of the bus headed for Madrid, and come back to her, in gentle remind. But there was nothing gentle at all about what she had done, and to the only one who had really loved her. This story did not belong to her, she thought. And yet there it sat, upon her, in her, all over her—how had she done this? This was not her life, this was not hers, this did not belong to her. As soon as she was off this stuffy bus, she would realize that it was fine, that everything was the way it had been and she would go on with her life as planned. "I'll go on with life as planned," she repeated to herself between gritted teeth, as her body began to shake and her heart began to beat very fast, and then suddenly not at all, it seemed. Cold sweat ran down her arms. She thought she would vomit, thought her stomach would fall out. The more she said it, *I will go on with my life as planned*, the worse the convulsions. It was as if her body knew the truth, and as if even her own limbs hated her for it. No, her life would not, could not go on as planned. And at that moment the immensity of what she had done and what she could not change came back to her. Most of all, more than the betrayal, more than the loss, she lamented that everything she had imagined about how her life would be, suddenly no longer was and would never be again. And with her entire body, she grieved that life was no longer a dream, a beautiful far away gem for the taking, but a small, sad plot.

Chapter 23

I DON'T REMEMBER what Regalado looked like then. Or what his voice sounded like. What made me go to him, what made me do that to Carmen. He was not handsome, he was not particularly kind. But there was that something, that thing you can't name and can't give up once you get it. Even as I carried you inside me, I knew I was powerless to destroy you who had come from him. It was a thing he carried, a way in the world that was not entirely at ease, but was unafraid, unhindered. Maybe it was because Rego did not care—because societal conventions didn't matter to him and he placed all his bets on what was in front of him at any moment. If he didn't come home for several nights in a row, he'd found something else that caught his interest. If he left Carmen for a rich Mexican on a fluke after 24 years, it was because Carmen was not in front of him and the rich Mexican was. It sounds fickle but there was something very attractive about not having any propriety in a world full of righteous assholes.

When the reporters would interview him after a new gallery exhibit opened, Regalado refused to give them what they wanted. "Why do you paint?" they'd want to know, and he'd answer, "What the hell do I know? I paint. I fuck. I sleep. How the hell do I know why?" And he was right—even though he was unfair that way, he was also right. You wouldn't think you'd fall in love with someone like that, or I didn't think I would. But he would turn on you, and suddenly all that gypsy machismo would go away and he'd be there looking at you with the straightest look anyone ever had. He'd remember everything you told him, every last detail. More than any silly teenage boyfriend ever had. He'd look at you and his eyes would peer down into you and hit you in that spot between your legs where you could not deny what he was doing to you.

No one had ever done that to me. I didn't even know it was possible for someone to look you in the eye and make you feel that way. If I try, I can still see him sometimes—sitting there next to me at Doña *Guadalupe's bar, with a hand-rolled cigarette in his fingers, his head cocked, seducing me with his pain. I wish I could go back and tell him—don't do this to me, don't make me feel this way, not with me. Go home to your woman, go to your* mujer, *make her feel that way, look at her that way. This I know for sure; I would go back and drop him off at Carmen's door and walk up the stairs to my apartment and never look back. Of course, if it hadn't been with me it would have been with some other woman—in fact, was. And if I'd done that, you would not have been born. But then, that summer of 1978, it was me—I was the girl who had never felt that knowing from deep inside, that she could not walk away. That I'd have to see it through to its nasty end. It felt too good to feel that savage man saying, I dare you. Come home with me,* vente conmigo.

I can't see his face anymore but I can hear those words, those salty, sweaty words slipping into my ear. I can feel myself, arrogant and naïve, leaving Jovi that night. I can feel my feet scurrying up the hill with him to his studio before anyone might see us. I can see the front door of his studio, the handle surely having been polished by Carmen herself earlier that week. I can see him lighting an oil lamp and a cigarette, peeling away my clothes while the smoke hung from his lips. What was it about the way he held a woman that made you ache and bleed and need so badly? That is how he held me that night. That is how he entered me—with his dark spirit, his black desire, his underworld of duende *pouring out of him into my hips. His arm circled around my back…nothing else existed outside that twin bed in his darkened studio. Not Carmen, not my father, not Zorita, not Franco, not Cuenca, not all of New York. Nothing, but that man's arms around me, pouring something into me that was not nameable.*

I wish that I could say each of the successive nights were like that first night, that the love we made was worth any price, any heartbreak. Maybe then somehow I could justify that I didn't do it once but several more times—each time aware I was doing a terrible thing, and unable—no, unwilling—to stop it for the hope it would be as good as it was that first night when Regalado tore me open and exposed me to the windy universe beyond. I could have told you how we met after midnight, after he'd had a late dinner with Carmen and kissed her and the dogs goodnight. I could have told you how we talked about the paintings that he was working on, how he'd pour us whiskey and play flamenco albums. I could have told you that although it was terrible what we did, that passion took us over and it had all been worth it.

But really, each time we met I felt more of the pretension of what I was doing; the role I was enacting took up more space, and the payoff got smaller.

Having a man's penis in your mouth is the surest way to know if you love him; it's the best test of whether what two people share is real or not. The last time I saw him, we were in Javier's huerta. *He was half drunk—as he nearly always was—splayed in the shade of an olive tree, the Spanish August heat oppressive around us. He unzipped his pants and took out his penis. Folding his sex into my mouth, I could smell the scotch on him, seeping through his skin. I looked up at him, and began to see him more clearly. The romanticism I'd felt that night at Soto's, dancing* sevillanas *with Regalado, was gone. Then I saw myself through his eyes. I knew then at best I had been just another* coño, *and at worst, a cruel game of his to hurt Carmen for sick reasons no one but the fascists who killed his father on the hill could understand.*

I sucked him off, swallowed his seed, and ran to the other side of the garden to vomit. He had already fallen asleep but I had woken suddenly from what I had done, had been doing. It occurred to me I might be pregnant. The thought I'd made this betrayal a permanent stain upon me made me vomit again. I left him there under the tree, let myself out of Javi's huerta, *and ran as quickly as I could—knowing I would never see him again, and knowing I would have to leave Cuenca that night. I could not stand to face Carmen again. I prayed she would never learn what I had done.*

I ran away from Regalado, *as if my limbs carried me...I ran up the mountain, to* San Isidro *cemetery where I'd come so many times on my walks over the past four months. It was early evening and a full moon rose over the mountaintops; the hills were lit up with an orange glow and you could hear music echoing off the mountain for miles. I walked through the gates of the burial grounds where a large group of people of all ages had gathered for a festival, the origins of which were unknown to me. At the center near the old stone fountain was a massive bonfire that a burly man covered in ash tended with a long fire iron; multiple other fires burned at our feet with piles of ash that glowed red; upon them butchers lay hinged grills containing blood sausage, pork ribs, and entrails.*

An old man stepped into the center of the circle, fires raging around him and began to sing. He sang humble but powerful notes, and the crowd took turns on the chorus, clapping hands. It went like this all night. The old men sang their wives love songs, the old women sang to their grandchildren, warning them of the love that would break them. I watched with envy at their community, their connectedness. I wanted to return to the way it was before this had all begun. Before I became a woman who had the seed of another woman's man growing inside her. Like I had been before. I wanted these bonfires with entrails spread across them to burn away my sins; to make it untrue.

I watched the strange and beautiful scene unfolding from the tombstones where Zorita's body would one day lie; they sang that night till their voices went hoarse and the wood had run out and the fires had dimmed; the faces, covered in ash went home. Zorita had sworn that Cuenca had something special and he had been right. There was an air in Cuenca that was different than any place I had been before. It came up from the mountains and left shivers down your spine. Something special, I won't say divine, but something mysterious lives in Cuenca—a magic that takes your breath away.

I laid myself out on one of the tombs and felt the still warm summer air brushing across my bare legs. I lay like that, without moving till almost dawn. I understood that I would never be able to take back what I had done. And somewhere in me, I knew that however it ended, Carmen would find out. With this knowledge sinking into my bones, I think that very night I felt my soul slip away. It was a faint sound, like a little sigh. You would think when a soul goes away it would be loud and clamorous. But no, mine went very quietly as the realization set in that I could take nothing back and it had all been for nothing.

That is the last memory I have of Spain. The next day I packed my things, and without telling Carmen or saying goodbye, I left on the night bus to Madrid.

Is this the story you wanted me to tell you? Is this the one you were waiting to hear?

When you look for your root—I want you to know the truth, but I do not want you to see this story. I want you to look to his cuadros, *his precious oil and canvas. Look there for your root. Look to his stained-glass windows that stud the cathedral walls with his anarchy and vision. Look to his understanding that this life is temporary and there is nothing that matters as much as the art we leave behind. Look to Carmen, the woman who tells his story, again and again even as he broke her heart again and again. Because she believed in him and loves him even today. You've heard my story now, you've heard her story. Hers has Basque melodies, salted cod, and gypsy blood. Let her be your root, now that he is gone, let her tell you why she loved him, let her show you his LPs, let her teach you how to grow rose geraniums, and how to see paintings in darkness. She lives to tell this story, and her story, my story is now your story, your blood, your root. This is all we have left, but it is all you have ever wanted. Take comfort in it,* hija mía.

Chapter 24

RAFAEL ACCOMPANIED ME back to Carmen's house. They knew each other well from the museum and Rafael had eaten many a meal at Carmen's kitchen table. He told me there was no doubt she knew which one of *El Grupo* my father was.

Carmen was waiting for us when we came back as if she'd known we'd be returning to learn more from her soon. As we entered the building and made our way up the stairwell, we could hear jazz music playing from Carmen's apartment. I knocked at her door.

After a moment we heard soft footsteps and the dog's barking, and the door opened. Carmen stood in the entry, several stairs below us, her loyal dog, Rocco by her side. The room behind her was dark, except for the lamp over Chillida's black and white print. Her white apron and silver bun made for an austere portrait. I realized this woman might hold the key to my roots, my origin, my father, *el pintor español.*

"*Pasa*," Carmen smiled softly and I began down the stairs to her apartment. Rafael followed me and they greeted each other, with Rafael giving a kiss on each of Carmen's cheeks.

The upstairs living room was a deep shade of blue. One chair sat separated from the table, directly facing a painting of Regalado's.

I sensed I would soon learn who my father was. I felt exposed and vulnerable here in this foreign place. But there was no choice now—the time had come to have this conversation.

Carmen remained standing in the almost dark room staring at the canvas on the wall. To break the silence, I pointed to the plant seated on a tall chair next to the painting, "What a view they have."

Carmen smiled softly and said, "You are just like your mother, you notice every detail. Of course you want to know about the plants. Your mother would not like the plants distracting from the artwork."

"You know my mother?"

Carmen smiled but did not answer my question as she continued:

"I moved the plant today. Let me explain...you see, there was a time when I would not have accepted a plant next to a painting, next to a masterpiece like this one. And this painting, it was a masterpiece, it was. Look at all those little details—the little birds, next to the bull's head, the phallic symbols. There's so much movement in it, so much energy. I love this painting. But you see, I have this plant and it needs light, and the light is best in that spot, right in front of the painting. There was a time when I would have said the life of a painting was more important than any plant. But I'm older now, and I take care of these plants. And I cannot deny a living thing the light it needs to live for the sake of a painting. Which is more important, the painting or the plant? I think now it is the plant."

I looked at Rafael, uncertain of what to say. He blinked his eyes gently. Carmen continued.

"I love your question. I love that only you and your mother would ask that question. Of course you want to know about the plant. Because paintings do not need decoration. And I do not like decoration for decoration's sake. But the light, that's where the plant thrives, so that is where I leave it." We stood in silence. Rafael finally stepped in to help.

"Carmen—Isabel has come here for a purpose. She believes her father may be one of *El Grupo*...We thought you might know who."

Without averting her eyes from the canvas, Carmen said to Rafael, *"Claro que lo conozco."* Of course I know him.

"You know him?" Rafael's hands flew up in the air and he looked at me with a smile. "This is incredible news! Who is it? You must tell us!"

Carmen took a deep breath and looked at me closely, then said something that nearly knocked me off my feet.

"Regalado Eneko. My husband."

I stood dumbly looking at Carmen as if the words she had said were some alien tongue that my brain could not decipher. Rafael was first to speak.

"Coño, ¿pero que dices, Carmen? ¿Que dices?"

"...Do not worry, I am an old woman on the outside but my heart is strong. I am no longer ashamed, and I am no longer afraid. I do not fear what you will think of me. Don't feel you need to protect me like I am an old woman. My first husband kept me like that, and I don't like it. I need to say what I feel and what I think."

Carmen pulled a chair out for me to sit on. She did not turn on the lights, but turned around to the armoire that held her records and stereo. She bent down, searching for an album in the dark in her stack of LPs. Rafael seated himself quietly in the corner, doing his best not to intrude.

"Here it is, here it is," she said as she took what I recognized to be a Thelonius Monk record from the player and replaced it with another album.

"I love Thelonius; Rego and I once saw him play in Paris. Genius. But this, this was your mother's favorite album when she was here. An old Spanish standard. *'Nosotros,' se llama*."

A melodic, instrumental track started, then a man and woman started singing together in Spanish. Carmen passed me the album cover. "Here, look at it." I took the album cover in my hands and turned it over.

"What is it Carmen?"

"Look in the corner. In the top right corner there." There in the corner, in a messy cursive read, *Regalado '76*. I swallowed hard.

"So now you know. Regalado was my partner of 24 years. And you are Rebecca's daughter. And also Regalado's."

I sat mute, bewildered, turned over by this revelation. Carmen looked me over, not unkindly; she appeared relieved to have acknowledged who we both were. I had no idea what to expect but was grateful Rafael was with me; it was intimidating to come up against a woman of her age and wisdom. I also still had no idea if or how angry she was with my mother. If my nerves were shattered, Carmen appeared somber but comfortable. She had been waiting for this day and she was in her element.

"What does your mother do now? Where is she?"

"We live in Los Angeles. She collects art for a museum, studies it. We don't get along very well."

"Ah, you don't understand each other," Carmen repeated softly, as if clarifying the point to herself.

"It is always a shame when mothers and daughters do not understand one another. It was the same for me with my mother. But it is tragic. In a way, it's tragic, isn't it?"

I nodded.

"But then, what would life be without these tragic things?" The dog had curled up next to Carmen's feet. She reached down to pat his head softly, then adjusted her white apron.

"*Ya*," she whispered under her breath, *Enough*.

"I will tell you things. I will tell you things of your father. Stories—that's what you've come for, isn't it?"

I looked at Rafael hopefully as Carmen, cloaked in darkness, surrounded by my father's paintings began to tell me the story that led me here. Rafael translated her words effortlessly:

"Everyone thinks that living life means spending all day outside, surrounded by people, and all that. But I want to live life right here. As the years go by, there are things you can't escape. Life has also taught me the things I can and cannot do, the things I can and cannot accept. I have learned I don't have any choice but to surrender. It's not easy to surrender when you do not believe in God. Who will be there on the other side? But I have always promised myself that if someday a door opened to me, I would walk through to the other side. *¿Sabes*? That was my promise…And then you appeared.

"*Sabes*, I am very different from others. *Muy particular.* For many years there were just three things I really loved, three things! Of course, not more than people—because you cannot love a thing as you can a person, of course that is clear. But there were three kinds of objects I loved. Can you imagine? Three very simple things: Well-ironed sheets, stacked white towels and Rego's paintings. I know the towels and the sheets are two simple things, two silly things really—especially when next to a work of art. But that's what I loved. When Rego was in Madrid or after he'd left, I'd stay up late in the kitchen, the windows wide open, some radio program from Granada playing an old Flamenco record as I ironed. I still use that kitchen table to iron on—it's better than any ironing board, I tell you. There's a trick to ironing, most people don't know; you see, if you don't let the clothes dry completely, and instead you put them in bags while they're still damp, it makes ironing much easier later. I used to do this with Rego's shirts, or the sheets. I loved hanging the bath towels from the window, still damp from the washer to dry in the moonlight. And of course, of course I loved his painting that hung on the wall over the kitchen table. There's a little beast in the corner, like I told you—he loved those little *bichos* in his paintings. They were small things, meaningless maybe, it's true. But it was my world, my kitchen was my universe. I gave my love to those bedsheets and the towels—I'd iron every last crease from his clothing till early hours. When I was done, I would sit with a cup of hot milk, my feet up on another chair, and I'd stare at his painting and the piles of clothes and folded towels stacked neatly on the table. And I tell you, I loved them equally, those stacks of clothes and his painting. It was as if at those moments the painting would look down and say, *Nice work, Carmen, nice work*. Then I'd fill my arms with the bedsheets and towels, turn off the kitchen light and tiptoe up the stairs to put them away and put myself to bed. Rego was not there these nights, and I loved how clean and quiet the house would be. And I'd hear the house, like the painting, whisper to me: *Nice work, Carmen, nice work*. What a fool I am! But yes, this is what I loved. I am, after all these years, a simple housewife. This is my world, these are the things I love.

"You must wonder what your mother was like then. I don't know her anymore, I don't know what she's like now. But I remember when she came to Cuenca, I can still see her getting off the train with Zorita, him hunched over from his scoliosis, and her, tall and thin, like a little bird. She had strawberry blonde hair, which made everyone stare at her. She used to think Spaniards were being cruel, but no, this was not it. They had seen so few women like her. A young American woman—a Jew of all things—she was like an alien to us! I remember wanting to get a good look at her before I had to say hello, wanting to see from afar whether we'd get along well. I remember how nervous I was when she and Zorita finally made their way across the platform to me. I told myself, *Quit it, Carmen, it's just an American girl!* But I was like everyone else in Spain…we were forty years behind the world. She represented, I don't know, something modern, something undiscovered. She had a simple loveliness about her, but she was so genuine, so curious, it made her quite beautiful.

"How I loved having her for lunch every Sunday. We talked every single day—either in the stairwell or over a coffee in the apartment. Not a day went by we didn't meet. I don't know what it was about Rebecca, but she got under my skin. There was a chemistry between us, a spark that is rare, very rare to find with someone else. If I had had a daughter of my own, I don't think I could have loved her more than I loved Rebecca.

"You should have seen how the dogs took a liking to her too—she was soft like that, and they felt it. She was so sweet, she almost disappeared a little. That was why she had to force Soto and the other painters to take her seriously. They couldn't imagine a young blonde girl from America had anything to teach them. But she did—she was very smart, your mother. And when they had ignored Zorita's demands to include her, she figured out how to get their attention. I knew I couldn't do it for her, but it was amazing to watch her reel them into her lap. Very smart she was.

"When she left…it was like a kick in the stomach. I didn't know why she had left, and I had just started to really imagine that we would be friends for many years—that she would come back to Spain over the years, that we'd write letters and talk by phone, that I would hold her babies. That she left so quickly, with no explanation made me think I had done something…that we hadn't treated her right. I didn't understand. I was heartbroken.

"Mercedes, Soto's wife finally told me what had happened. The whole town knew, they knew about how Regalado had danced with your mother at Soto's, how they had gone off together that night. It was poor Mercedes who was left to tell me, also when word came that she was pregnant with his child. She had tried to keep it from me, but she could not help herself, she was full of guilt about it. 'Carmen,' she said, 'You know the girl is pregnant. Regalado told Soto he heard from her. He is making like it is not his child, but Carmen, I—I just thought you should know.'

"What could I say? It was humiliating. Mercedes urged me to leave him then and there. It wasn't the first time he had done this to me, I won't pretend that. I knew there had been other women. But this had been in my face, with a girl who was like a daughter to me. She was so young—I should have guessed Regalado would have some *borrachera* and go after her.

"Regalado and I, we were an older couple by then. Me well past middle age, thinking that we were building something more mature, that we'd be able to grow older together. Mercedes wanted me to leave him. Even Soto who loved Rego said, 'Carmen, come on, he doesn't deserve you anymore.'

"After Rebecca had gone and I knew all that had passed, he came home crying to me and he was like a little child. He apologized, crying and shaking in my arms. And I thought…I thought I could forgive him. He was so lost, he was so turned inside out, he didn't think about anyone else, he just felt tortured…it was as if he needed to spread the pain that lived in him around to others. I knew that—I had known that when I left Juan for him.

"I tried to forgive him and you know, move on and let go of Rebecca's leaving and what had happened. I did for a while, maybe for awhile I did forgive him. But you know, old dogs, they don't change. And Regalado, within a few months had forgotten the mess he'd left behind. But I knew…I knew that your mother was pregnant and alone in the United States. I know it's crazy, but I could hear her from across the ocean. And I knew she was in pain. She suffered badly, I could feel it. Sometimes I would wake in the morning and it was as if she was right there with me. I could hear her talking to me as sometimes the living do to the dead. She cried and cried through her pregnancy with you, I knew that, eh? She'd ask me what I was making that day for lunch, and I'd almost answer her. Again and again I'd hear your mother telling me, in heavy tones, *lo siento, lo siento.* I knew she had loved me, and that made it all worse.

"It is not a pretty story, my child. Do you know though, do you know why we loved him? Because I've told you this story—about your mother, about Rego, about what he did, about what happened. But what I didn't tell you was why I loved him. I have not told you that he was not only part drunk, part gypsy, part beast, but a man, a tender, tender man, with the deepest soul I have ever seen. I did not tell you how the same man, who would return nearly every night drunk and angry at life, would also turn my body from bone and cell and skin to earthen soil with the most gentle gesture or touch. He painted monsters, demon-like horrible creatures, *¿sabes?* You've seen his paintings...but in the corner of the canvas, a bird that sang.

"You should have seen him, he used to handle simple objects like little children. And he knew the names of birds. And insects. He cooked rice better than any homemaker in Spain. He liked to play drums, though no one had taught him. He sat without a word for hours at the window, or lying in bed between masturbation and television, then suddenly would get an idea and would disappear for days to paint in the studio. He called everyone he met by some tender nickname. He took friends who were ugly and had no way with women to brothels and coaxed them out of their awkwardness. To make love with him was to know laughter, silence and joy. Pure joy. He made it hard for us later. But he was not hard to love. One evening at a table with him over wine and *bacalao* and you loved him, you simply did. Man or woman, you loved him. It was not his dark eyes or thick hair. He did not smile beautifully—his teeth were crooked and yellowed from tobacco. But he opened up worlds. Not just doors to worlds but an entire universe of planets you'd never imagined could exist. To look at art or even a teacup, and hear how in a word he'd change your view of it forever, was to love him.

"He was the painter, but I was his witness. Morning and night I watched him. I watched him as if he were a precious, exotic jewel I had found in my pocket by chance one day. I watched him like I used to watch the water as a little girl in San Sebastián. I knew when his tides came and went, and what a certain look in the waves meant—there would be a storm coming. He was as vast and blue as that sea and like the sea I could not move my vision from him. There was nowhere else to look when he was before me. In some ways, my life did not begin until I met Rego. Even after he'd left with the Mexican, and I was torn apart, I knew my life would become closed and small without him. So I watched him. Sometimes like a biologist looks at an unknown creature. Mostly I watched him with love. I don't know, maybe he watched me too. Maybe he knew my lines and veins and marks like I knew his. If he did, he never told me."

What was left of the light outside had faded. Carmen stood up and lit a candle on the long table we sat around. Neat stacks of art books and catalogues covered the surface. Rafael and I had barely moved as Carmen had spoken. Again, we waited for her direction. Carmen adjusted a painting on the wall, folded her apron around her, and sat down again to continue with her story.

"Isabel, I've never told anyone about how it ended with your father. I want to tell you—because I promised if ever the daughter of Regalado and Rebecca came looking for him, I would tell her everything. It will not make you love him more—it's a terrible, terrible story. And your father, as much as I loved him, and as much as I know he loved me—and I know he loved me very much, he did some terrible things to me. Everyone knows about the drinking, that was awful, it's true. There were also affairs; there were women before your mother, and there were women after. I put up with it because I knew above all, Regalado came home to me, and that he loved me more than any of them. I looked a few of them in the eye—one of them he even brought home and screwed all night in the upstairs bedroom. It's why I have my bedroom down here next to the kitchen, now. I still can't bear to sleep up there. But this last time, it was different. Regalado had already started slipping away a bit after the summer with your mother…he started sleeping more, started spending more and more time at the studio up the hill or in Madrid, at his studio there. It didn't happen all of a sudden, maybe it had been happening a long time…it was small at first, so I didn't notice till it happened with your mother, and I realized things had changed between us. It was as if he had gotten smaller and smaller over the years, more petty, you know? Maybe it was the drugs, maybe it was the *borracheras*. It was as if he was only half alive, half there. As if his human shell had been emptied out in the middle of the night. I tried to think what had happened, I tried to talk with him, but Regalado was impossible to talk to about these things. His paintings had started to sell well and we were earning good money, what with my salary and his. But I was more and more sure every day that he was disappearing from me. Like his soul had disappeared, out through the windows into the street, and into the glasses of whiskey he drank at *Doña* Guadalupe's counter, or in the *barrio* San Antón. It sounds crazy, but that's how it felt, that's how I saw it.

"I thought the drinking would get better. Or maybe I didn't know how bad it was; it took me a long time to realize all these things. I used to wait for him at night. . .if he did not come after dinner, I knew it meant he was out drinking and would come back and do terrible things. I used to wait for him and if he did not return, I would have a coat and scarf ready by the door and I would leave for the night. I knew his *borrachera* was brewing in some bar's basement in town. Zorita had left me his keys to look after his apartment while he was away. So I learned to be gone before the bars closed. I would take my things and leave our apartment, hoping no one would see me and ask where I was going. I would walk up the hill to Zorita's apartment and I would let myself into his gate and into his little garden flat. I never slept or even so much as sat down those nights but at least I would not have to face Regalado's drunken madness. It would come, for sure. But I stopped being there to hear it, to live through it. To beg him to stop only pushed him forward. It took me 14 years to learn that. 14 years of *locuras*. Fourteen years of broken plates, furniture thrown from the windows and our TV chopped to pieces. There was no point in fighting him like this. He was like an angry child—you just had to close the shutters and wait for things to calm down. It was like that and then I would return in the morning, he'd be in bed drawing. The house would be a disaster. He once threw a honey pot against the kitchen wall and it took weeks of peeling honey off the walls till it was clean again. He never asked where I had been and I did not ask how the honey got on the wall. He would just say to me, without looking up from his drawing, 'I am a son of a bitch.'

"He had always kept strange hours, he slept and woke 'like a gypsy,' my mother would have said. And he did. Late nights and long stretches without any sleep at all. But he had never slept through the day much, even after a *borrachera.* I started finding him at noon curled up in bed like a child who had caught a cold. I couldn't wake him, and I gave up trying because he'd turn mean as if he'd been out all night with a bottle of whiskey. I don't know even now what bit him, if it was drugs or booze or if he had what Andrés Padilla had, melancholy, you know. I don't know what it was, but for many years we had had something together, and slowly, we started not to anymore. Slowly he began to disappear from me.

"So I shouldn't have been surprised when all this happened... you know, we were never bound by marriage...I say my *husband* and everyone in Cuenca assumed we were married. But we had never been able to marry because divorce was illegal in Spain until after Franco died. Every time I bought a piece of property, Juan had to sign the papers—for thirty years it was like that, till Franco died and they started changing the laws. I bought all the property in my name, because at the time I had the money and was working regularly at the *posada.* I've never believed in a god, but when all this finally passed with Regalado, I think there was a god looking out for me. If we had been married, it all would have gone to him. Regalado would have taken me for all I was worth. He would have taken everything.

"It was about six years after your mother had gone—you would have been, what, five years old? I hadn't seen Regalado at home for over a week. I'd called the studio in Madrid, the art gallery, the corner bar there. No sign of Rego. Then Milagros, Esperanza's one-armed sister who ran the store sometimes, let it slip while I was buying my daily bread. She told me, '—*Eh, Carmen, no hay que comprar el pan.* Regalado already bought a loaf this morning.' From the look on my face, Milagros must have realized she'd said something she shouldn't have. I caught myself though, to keep from being humiliated and pretended everything was normal. '*Claro*,' I said, 'but I'm making a stew, so we'll need extra bread.'

"I didn't want Milagros to see the shame on my face. They'd know it, he'd cheated again and as always, I was the last to know. The grocers, the bar men, the curators, they all knew what Rego was up to and no one said a word to me. They said nothing. How ridiculous I must have looked…I was so mad I could barely breathe. I walked the groceries up the four flights of stairs and into our home. I was so mad I was swearing over and over with each step, '*¿qué coño? ¿qué coño?*' and it grew louder and louder until it exploded from my lips and I banged my fist on the kitchen table, like this, '*Su puta madre, ¿qué coño?!!*'

"I untied my apron and took it off. Once I'd regained my composure, I walked slowly and methodically out the door of our home and down onto the street. None of these assholes would look at me, would dare tell me what they all knew. That Regalado was a lying cheating *hijo de puta* and they all let him be. I would not give them the satisfaction of seeing my rage, of seeing my hands trembling inside my skirt pockets. I was shaking all over but I made sure to walk more slowly than usual. Almost as if I was meditating, as calm as the *monjas* in their black robes saying the rosary. That's how slowly I walked, just to defy them.

"Whatever woman he was holed up with this time, the bastard would have to look me in the eye and tell me himself what was going on. So I walked up the hill to the studio. It was the oldest building in town, aside from the old jail the city had turned into an archive. The iron door was the same one from 300 years earlier. Only the intercom had been added. I stood there, you know, willing him to not be there. Let Milagros be wrong, I thought, *que no sea cierto.* Don't let this be true again.

"But even as I willed it, I knew he was up there. I could see the shutters were slightly ajar and I knew Milagros had not been mistaken; I had seen the look on her face—and if Regalado was in Cuenca, but hadn't been home for a week, there was only one reason why. I took a deep breath then unlocked the portal and marched up the stairs. I did not stop to turn on the hall lights, I walked up in the dark, till I got to his studio door at the top of the stairs; I had my key ready and flung the door open. Whatever woman was in there, whoever it was this time, I had to know.

"I could smell the musty floors, taste the oil in the room. And there he stood at his *máquina.* The marvelous printing machine I'd helped him build and make thousands of prints from over the years. His face showed nothing. He just kept turning the gears as the paper moved through the large metal rollers. A cigarette hung from his lips and his hair was a mess. He looked like a terrible beast to me, untamed, unaware except of his own survival. I stood there waiting for this beast to look up, to acknowledge me, to say something, *coño*—anything. But he just smoked his cigarette and tended to his print.

'Ey,' I called to him. "What are you doing here?" Only the *máquina* replied, its grr grr grrr sound of metal pressing paint. 'Ey, don't you see that I am here? You haven't called or been home in a week. What is with you?'

"Still just silence and the *máquina.* That stupid *máquina*! The phone rang and I could feel my blood rising as Rego went to pick it up. He still had not so much as looked at me. I saw his hand move for the receiver and I nearly jumped the length of the room, I was on him so fast. My hand slammed down over his on top of the phone. He pulled his hand back, surprised by my anger. I had never so much as raised my voice to him. I hurled the phone to the other side of the room, and snapped, 'Now you are talking to me. And you won't talk to anyone else until we are finished.'

"But Rego just stood there smoking, he had the cruelest look on his face I'd ever seen. So I repeated myself, and I said,

'What the hell is going on? Why have you not been home in a week? I was worried sick, I called everywhere, in Madrid, I called Soto—no one will tell me what is going on.'

'What do you want?'

'I want you to talk to me. To tell me what is going on.'

'Don't you know by now?'

'Know what? Is there another woman? Is that it?'

'Woman, do you not see that I don't love you anymore?'

"He said it without so much as looking up from the *máquina*. I felt my whole body snap and go completely limp. I'd expected to find a woman here, maybe catch them in bed, but not this. I had survived his drunken, violent rages, his betrayal, his absence. I never said a word—not a word! Because I had chosen this life. I had left Juan for Regalado. I knew even then, almost 30 years before, that this life would not be easy or simple. But he'd always promised me his love. It had carried me through every dark day and night. And now this? To be shut out of his love and affection like a common whore? I saw him look up from the *máquina* for a moment, I could see he pitied me. He, the drunk, pitied me! He did not so much as blink. Then he turned back to his *máquina.*

"Three days later, Regalado emptied out our home and savings account while I worked at the *posada.* He told the bank manager he was taking me on a trip to Buenos Aires. He took everything. *Everything.*

"I didn't think till that day he left about what I had given up for him. I didn't think during 30 years of violent rages, not as we built a home, not as I made him lunch and dinner, not as I waited for him to come home, about what I had given up. But that night, after I'd come home to find the house like that, *coño,* even the television gone, I sat in my kitchen, on the floor and I cried so hard the house shook. I started making a list, of all the dreams I had put away for him. I never started my own restaurant—even though it was proposed to me many times. I had not so much as cut my hair another length. I had worked as a cleaning lady to pay for his oil paints. And most of all, I'd never had children with Rego because I had seen the way he treated the dogs when he was drunk. I could not have lived with myself if we had had a child and he had taken a hand to them. Everything I had done I had done for him. His needs had always come first. And this is how he had left me…He didn't take the dog, thank god. And the dog, he didn't leave my side for weeks, he knew how bad off I was."

Carmen looked up at Rafael and me sitting silently in the darkness. We knew without saying so that this was the first time she'd ever told this story. There was little we could do to ease the pain except listen. We knew we had to bear witness to her story. I could not take away the pain my mother or Regalado had caused this woman who had loved them both more than anyone in the world. But I sensed hearing her was a kind of healing. It was all I had to give her of any value.

"It isn't the life I'd imagined for myself when I had left Juan, but you know...even after all that, after everything terrible he made me live through, Regalado is still the only man I have ever loved, and the only man I could bear to be with..."

Carmen took a deep breath and then looked at me squarely in the eye.

"...And now you've come."

"Carmen, I am so sorry. I had no idea."

"Sorry? You have done nothing to me. You have nothing to excuse yourself for."

"Then I am sorry for my mother. It was wrong what she did, and I—"

Carmen cut me off:

"*Sabes*, I am not angry with your mother anymore. You see, Regalado did many more despicable things other than sleep with a young woman from America. It wasn't her fault. He was the adult, she was our responsibility. He took advantage of that. It wasn't right. I don't blame your mother. I did for a long time, but she was young and we do stupid things when we are young that we regret for the rest of our lives sometimes. Those years after your mother left, and then after Rego did, they were the hardest years of my life. I didn't know that I could get through them, that I could survive. I didn't know I could survive without Regalado. The first three years, they were the worst. There were days and weeks I did nothing but go to work and lie in bed. But then, after a few years, I found I was still alive. I was still there, me, Carmen. I said to myself, Carmen, you have to accept this now.

"I started to live again, a little. I found rituals that belonged to me, things I liked to do—like listen to music in the dark, or walk with the dogs *por el monte.* Things I had never had time to do before Regalado left. I paid my dues with Rego, you know? I would do it again, I would—I know it sounds crazy, but I would. I never stopped loving Rego to this day. But you know, now that so many years have gone by, I would not take him back. I would have those first few years. But now, I could not…He tried—do you know that? He came back twice and asked me to take him back. One time he had a friend bring him from Madrid and they picked me up in their limo and he tried to talk his way back into our home. Another time he begged me over the phone to take him back.

"The Mexican he married left him broke, like he had left me, once she realized what a pain he was. He knows that no one took better care of him than me. I saw to everything—that he had the best food, the cleanest clothes, that he was loved like no woman had ever loved him—not even his mother.

"I will never love another man again, but I respect myself too much to give my life back to him."

Chapter 25

Carmen rubbed the fish with olive oil. She took a clove of garlic and smashed it with the palm of her hand on the counter. So that's where my mother had learned that. The action always hurt my palm but my mother had sworn by it. "That's how you get the flavor out," she'd told me when she saw me using the garlic press. And now here was a 74-year-old Spanish woman I was not related to, telling me the same thing.

"*Con fuerza*." She repeated this slowly, showing me the garlic and holding up her palm for emphasis. "*¿Eh? Con fuerza*."

We had let Carmen tell her story until she was empty. Then she suggested we eat.

"But anyway," she said, trying to lighten the mood, "We can't live on stories, can we?"

We laughed and wiped tears from our eyes. I felt raw, like I'd been cut up in pieces and glued back together. The room was heavy from the listening. *We can't live on stories, can we?* It reminded me of Omar, telling me I could not live on Snickers and hash. For a moment, I missed him and his earthy embrace. *I could use your strength about now*, I thought.

The three of us descended into the kitchen, Carmen poured wine, and went to work making us dinner. I watched Carmen remove the skin off the clove and then rub the white fleshy fish down with garlic.

"All you need are four things in the kitchen, *eh*, Isabel? Four things. Aside from salt, of course."

"What four things are those?"

Rafael chimed in, "Let me guess—at least two I know: garlic, and olive oil?"

"Yes, very good Rafael. What are the other two?" Carmen asked us playfully.

"I'm going to go with Manchego?" I conferred with Rafael in English.

"Don't think I don't understand your English!" Carmen said, laughing. "Actually, I understand almost nothing! It always sounds like nonsense to me!"

"Okay, *cuatro cosas*..." said Rafael returning to Carmen's quiz. "Lemon?"

"Yes, lemon is the third, of course. And?"

"I know!" I shouted. "Parsley!"

"Very good!" Carmen encouraged me. "But I think you cheated," she said, pointing to a glass on the counter with a bunch of parsley.

"I just used my skills of observation is all," I said to Rafael in English, smiling. "Can you translate skills of observation for me?" Rafael repeated what I'd said to Carmen in Spanish and she laughed.

"Yes, you painters have that in common," Carmen paused, and a heaviness returned to the kitchen.

"Isabel, I'm sorry I didn't tell you who I was when we met. I knew right away when I saw you at Esperanza's. When you came, I said, *Carmen, this is your chance.* This is your chance to make it right again with Rebecca, regardless of what pain Regalado caused. You looked so much like her, your expressive eyes, your manner. And I could see Regalado in you too. From the minute I saw you, I knew. Standing there at Esperanza's shop, looking at me, so hopeful. After all these years I didn't want you to disappear, I didn't want to lose my chance to see your mother again. It was wrong of me—a terrible thing to do, terrible. *¿Lo ves*? I am flawed too, I am no saint. I couldn't have lived with Regalado all those years if I was just an innocent party. I went along with so many things out of love for him, or because I was too afraid to make my own choices. But either way, I was complicit, too. Do you understand?

"There are many things I would do differently if I had to do them over again. Your father never regretted much in his life—it's what made him so beautiful and such a brute. He just did things, paf! Like he painted, paf! He'd strike something into his life, or out of it. He'd paint a masterpiece or chop the TV in half. Paf! That was Regalado. Do not hate him for it, promise me? Promise me you will try to understand the context he came from. It would be sad for you to be angry with him now for those things he did."

"Where is he now?"

The question erupted from me almost involuntarily. I regretted the tone in my voice that sounded impatient—and I didn't want her to think that I didn't value this time with her. The truth was, spending only a few hours with Carmen had given me more insight into my father than 20 years with my mother! But I still didn't know where my father was, or if I would ever see him. I could not relax until I knew where to find him.

"*Bueno*, Isabel." Carmen turned from the stove where the fish was gurgling in a mixture of butter and garlic. Carmen looked at me hard but did not flinch.

"Regalado—your, *your father*—is not well. He is at a clinic in Madrid…Isabel, he is dying."

Chapter 26

After dinner, I said goodnight to Carmen and Rafael and excused myself for some fresh air. I grabbed my sketchbook, let myself out of Carmen's building and headed north. I walked up through the old town, past the *Plaza Mayor*; past the tables set out for the tourists and old ladies having their evening cocktails, past the monastery with the nuns who'd taken a vow of silence; past the *Posada*; past the *Hotel de Leonor*; past three churches that had fallen into disrepair. I didn't understand this place, didn't understand how I fit here, how I'd come from here. I was headed for the hills, but there was one stop I needed to make first.

I passed through the ancient outer city gate, a two-foot thick, twenty-foot high wall made of rock and crumbling limestone mortar. Rafael had told me when we were at the *Fundación* how Regalado's studio still sat on the other side of the *Castillo* wall. Hundreds of years ago, this wall marked the outer limits of the city—and together, with Cuenca's steep cliffs on all sides, this wall protected the villagers of Cuenca from invasion. It would be just like Regalado to have chosen a studio on the wrong side of the castle wall. I thought of him in his studio 300 years ago…from the stories Rafael and Carmen had told me, his likely would have been the anarchist gypsy house, welcoming the wanderers, the prostitutes, and the other undesirables with salted cod and home brewed beer. This thought pleased me; I understood why Carmen and my mother had loved him.

On the other side of the old archway stood a squat two story building with no markings or address—just a 12-foot-wide wooden door and windows covered tightly with wooden shutters and iron grilles. From the outside, it looked like any other building.

I walked up slowly to the door, as if I could find my father inside, waiting for my visit. My hand reached up and I pressed my palm against the wood. Leaning in to the door, I whispered as if reciting a prayer, "Can you hear me? I am here…Now I know it's you, Regalado. I've come to see you. I won't keep you, I promise. I just want to see you, just once." Only silence. I stepped back, then noticed something to the left side of the doorway—it was a buzzer with the names of the apartment occupants.

Lupe - 1°A and 1°B

Alfredo - 2°A

Regalado - 2°B

There it was—his name, typed so neat and unassuming on a little square of white card stock inside a plastic frame.

Regalado - 2°B

Tracing the length of his name along the call box, I pressed the button and could hear it ring somewhere upstairs, behind the big, ancient wooden door. I rang it twice more, feeling how bittersweet it was to be able to finally touch something of this man I had learned was my root, and yet be so far from him. I made a mental note to ask Carmen if I could return here, to see his paint brushes, his unfinished canvases. Rafael had told me Carmen had not touched the place since he'd gone. It had sat locked up for over a decade. I walked backwards into the deserted street, took out my paper and pencil and sketched a quick drawing of the building, with its ancient door. *What secrets you could tell,* I thought.

I turned then and headed for the hills. I walked and walked that night—as the moon rose and the darkness lengthened. I walked along the side of the winding road that led to Madrid, until I had left the town and could see the whole of Cuenca behind me. It looked so small from here. I tried to imagine my mother down there, twenty years before, and what she had done to create so many secrets and so many lies. And now I knew the story that she'd spent my life hiding from me. Who was she down there, twenty years old and making a lover of a painter three times her age?

Carmen had not wanted me to go. She had told me the man I would see at a hospice in Madrid was not the man I should remember. She warned me he would be a shell of a human being. *Deaf and dumb corpse* were the exact words Rafael had translated.

"He has forgotten how to paint, he is dying in a hospital room. I don't want that to be the man you remember," she pleaded with me. But it was no use. I had come here for one reason—to meet my father. Whatever the consequences, I'd come here to see him, and I could not wait another day to try.

I left Carmen's and made my way to the bus station to catch the next bus to Madrid. The Madrid station was minutes from Omar's hostal. I woke the next morning in his bed.

Fucking him had done me good. I needed to shake off this crazy story. These people…my mother, Carmen…my father. They were so fucked up! All of them! My mother's incredible narcissism, to have done that to Carmen…Regalado's insane ego…Carmen who put up with more than any human ever should. I hated all of them. And I loved them, terribly. No wonder my mother had not wanted me to come here. No wonder she'd shut me out of this history till I forced the matter.

And here I was again, in this place that had begun to break me open. He had welcomed me without question or comment at his door at midnight. I had taken the same bus that had delivered my mother from Cuenca to Madrid, as she fled Carmen's home with me growing in her belly. Omar ran a bath for me in the green tiled tub and fed me homemade *crema catalana.* I was grateful for his tub, for his loving, but mostly for his acceptance; how he knew not to ask more of me than I could give. He didn't ask when I had left if or when he would see me again, and this time, he didn't ask where I had been or what I had learned. He saw the sadness in my eyes, and that was all he needed to know. He bathed me, laid me down on his bed, and went down on me; he made me orgasm till I'd forgotten all of it and slept soundly. I blushed thinking of it as I got out of bed and went to find him, sheets wrapped around me like his desert queen.

Chapter 27

THE HOSPITAL WAS an eight-story concrete block building on the outskirts of Madrid. Carmen had reluctantly given me the name of the clinic and Regalado's room number. Omar had dropped me off with a hug and a fistful of *pesetas*. He told me to bribe the hospital staff if I had any trouble. But I hardly needed them; no one could stop me now. A security guard had me sign in and then directed me to the sixth floor. I made my way up the elevator, across several wards; the green linoleum seemed endless. A sea of doors and gurneys separated me from my father. I made a right turn down another corridor, trying to pretend I was just any other Spaniard visiting her ailing grandfather.

And then I heard it:

"*Tengo frío, tengo frío.*" An old man's garbled voice emerged from a room behind me.

"I am cold," the voice said again. I heard an echo of the words my mother had sworn to me, "*There is no future with him.*" I knew that it must be Regalado.

A nurse walked swiftly down the hall in the direction of the room where my father lay. She saw me hovering outside his room as I stood trying to decide how I could just walk in and say *hello-I'm-your-daughter* to a dying man who wouldn't know me or care that I'd come. The nurse eyed me suspiciously then shut the door swiftly between us. I could hear her saying to my father loudly, patronizingly, as if he were just a child, "*Está bien, tranquilo*, it's okay." I looked at the door and there it was, just like the studio, just like on his records and canvases: "*Room 608. Regalado Eneko.*"

I stood in the hall dumbfounded, staring at the brown hospital door that separated me from my father. I thought of my journals, pasted with traces of him and his art, his land that was Spain. I thought back to that night when this had all begun for me; that night I found my mother crying before the painting of the bull. I thought in anger of all the years my mother had wasted in letting me learn the truth...and now it was too late. Carmen was right. It had been a mistake to come to Madrid. The man named Regalado was still alive, but he lived no more. This was no time or place for a reunion. I stood motionless, the linoleum sticky beneath me.

"*¡Tengo frío, tengo frío!*" How could I ever forget the death rattle of my father?

I emerged from the clinic into the midday Madrid sun, tears streaming down my face, the sound of my father's tobacco-tinged voice from the hall outside his hospital room, "*Tengo frío, tengo frío*" repeating in my head, over and over again. The world seemed to be swimming around me, or maybe it was me swimming through a sea of grubby pavement and sick Spaniards. I could not stop crying, and I did not want to. I called Carmen from a dirty pay phone outside the clinic.

Carmen didn't even say hello, she just said my name.

"Isabel? Is that you?"

I could not reply, the tears choked my breathing and only little gasps came out.

"This is a mess we've put you through, all of us. You hear me? This is not your fault, you do not deserve this."

"I just wish I could have met him. That's all I wanted, was to know him. For him to know me."

"*Ay, mi niña.* I know. I am sorry. Listen to me, you must go to San Sebastián. That is where your father and I met. Our home is there. His books, his paintings. Will you go? Do you understand? Go meet your father in a place he will never grow old, meet the man I loved and who your mother knew. Isabel. *Vete a San Sebastián.*"

I was not ready to go back to Cuenca and even Omar's bed wasn't enough reason to stay in Madrid. I needed to go—away from Carmen, away from Cuenca, away from my mother's original sin that made me.

"Okay, okay," I said between tears, unable to summon Spanish up to talk.

"*Señor* Mariñelarena, our oldest friend is there, he will meet you and look after you. He is waiting for you now."

"Carmen… it hurts, I am so sad."

"Isabel—there are things, things that occur in life that you cannot take back. I would if I could—your mother would if she could have. Even Regalado, I believe he would take some of it back. But then you wouldn't be here. We cannot change the past. All we can do is to live through the pain. Go to San Sebastián. Watch the Sea of *Donostia* beat against the rocks. Do you hear me? Look, there, the sea crashes like no place else in the world. *Vete a nuestra tierra.* That is our home. Go to our earth, go to our bay, go to *Donostia* and find your father there. When you return to Cuenca we will start over."

I did as Carmen told me. There wasn't much else to do.

Chapter 28

I TOOK A cab to the station where Carmen had instructed me a bus would take me out of Madrid, stop in Bilbao, and pull into San Sebastián a few hours later. Carmen gave me *Señor* Mariñelarena's name and address. I had little idea of what awaited me there, but I had nowhere else to go. I sat in my seat, exhausted from the events of the past week since I'd left France. It felt like a lifetime already. Old ladies wearing aprons similar to Carmen's boarded the bus in twos. I buried myself in my sketchbook. The driver made a final passenger count and then we were off, rolling out of the dingy Madrid station, the gypsy women shaking their fists of rosemary at us one last time as if we might still de-board and buy from them.

I was grateful to leave Madrid. There was little for me here but an aging Moroccan lover and a dying man who would never speak my name. I had no future with either of them. *Qué pena*, I thought, the words in Spanish coming to me before the English ones. *What a shame.* As I said it, I realized for the first time ever I was speaking to my father. Not pretending or rehearsing, but actually speaking to him.

What a shame it had to be this way. I would have liked to have known you. I would have liked for you to have known me.

I woke hours later as the bus was driving into San Sebastián. The city was as Carmen had promised me it would be: Like Paris had been born in Spain. It was smaller than Paris, of course, but it had a distinctly different feel to it than Cuenca or Madrid. The streets were kept neatly, the shops a little less worn. The women were thinner, the old men proudly wore sailor's caps. I watched two men in hats, standing on the sidewalk, sharing a drink from the walkup window of a bar. *Any place with a walk-up bar window cannot be half bad*, I thought with a smile.

The bus pulled into the parking lot of the train station and let us off with a sigh. I had a note with the street address of Carmen's home here and cab fare to get there.

"You American?" The driver asked as we made our way across the bridge into the old town.

"Is it that obvious?"

"I noted your accent. The Americans, they go crazy in this city. Have you been here before?"

"My first time."

"Well then...You have to try the *chipirones*. You'll die for them, that's what we do here. The Basque, we know our fish."

"So I hear. A Basque friend sent me."

"Ah, you have a Basque friend! Well then, she will have told you all about us. Just eat a lot of fish, a lot of *pintxos* and you'll have a good stay," He laughed as he stopped the taxi.

"Here we are, *Calle Ibárruri, número 17?*"

"Yes, that's it."

A thin old man with white hair stood with a cane in the doorway of the apartment. From the looks of it, that was *Señor* Mariñelarena, the man Carmen told me would provide a key to the house. He must have been waiting for over an hour—my bus had not come in on time. I bid the taxi off and approached the old man. In a garbled Spanish I could barely understand he said:

"You are Isabel?"

I nodded.

"This way."

With that *Señor* Mariñelarena set off. He walked slowly down the sloped cobblestone street towards a smaller one just beyond the apartment house where he had been waiting for me. We walked in silence. I followed him like this through several winding alleys, each one narrower than the last, the walls of the apartment buildings just arms-width apart. We emerged and I found myself standing directly in front of a disquiet sea with a little house overlooking the black waves behind us. No wonder he had waited for me at the apartment building; there was no car access to the house we had come to.

"Here we are, here we are," *Señor* Mariñelarena announced, his gaze focused intently on his cane.

"Ah, the keys—here they are. Carmen said to make yourself at home. My wife cleaned it the other day. She'll bring by some wine and something for you to eat later."

I thanked *Señor* Mariñelarena and accepted the keys. Then he was gone, swept away by the stone pathways that had brought us here. I looked up to see a modest two-story house. Bright blue shutters and a blue door marked the facade with little bursts of color. Ceramic tiles covered the roof in a cape of muted red. There were no flowers or shrubs, just the dark blue ocean framing the house on either side. I followed a crumbling stone pathway up a small hill to the front door, clutching the key *Señor* Mariñelarena had left with me. It was an old-fashioned skeleton key—something that looked like it belonged to a castle or jailhouse from 100 years ago.

I inserted the key into the lock and opened the door. It was like stepping back in time. The floor was made from a dark wood and the walls were covered with bookshelves. The front room had a fireplace on the far right wall, and a small table and chairs. The only light came in from the front door and a narrow strip of light from a hallway at the end of the room. A long hall led past a kitchen and bathroom to a room made of windows. The sun was setting, a big orange ball sinking into the green sea that stretched into infinity. Two wooden chairs faced the sea, and a drafting table stood in the corner, pages of a drawing left mid sketch, as if it had been interrupted only moments before. I felt the moisture curling around my fingers. I closed my eyes and breathed in deeply, smelling the salt of the sea. I said a thanks for Carmen—after everything, here she was taking care of me.

I left my things and set out for a walk before darkness set in. It did not take long to confirm the sea was as wild as Carmen had promised. She was not exaggerating one bit; the waves were not the highest, but they were as fierce as any I had seen in California. I wrapped my scarf around me tightly and walked along *Paseo Eduardo Chillida* to his beloved "Wind Comb" sculpture. The massive shapes emerged from the rocks where the sea pounds the stone and iron morning and night. Two boys stood atop the rocks watching the waves crash against Chillida's creation. The bay behind us was protected from the wind and sea, but here, it was as if we were at the edge of the world. The boys howled in delight as each wave crashed, their arms outstretched to the salty spray of the sea. It took all I had in me to walk away; the sea was hypnotizing. But a storm was picking up and dinner called; I hadn't eaten since Omar had fed me soft-boiled eggs and toast that morning.

I was two miles from town without an umbrella when the rain began to fall hard from the still-light sky. I had no coat, no umbrella, and must have looked like a strange beast. I ran with abandon, laughing as I went till I found shelter beneath a cafe's canopy where others had already gathered to escape the downpour. I made my way between them, as if I was one of them; they barely noticed me as I sidled next to the gas heater to warm my hands, the thunder rolling itself out across the illuminated sky. I looked down at myself, my clothes were soaking wet, my hair was matted, the sketchbook in my bag was damp from the rain. And yet, I felt something peculiar inside me; as I had that first day in Cuenca. It was faint at first, then I felt it growing stronger as the rain poured down in sheets around us. And then I knew. That lightness in my stomach and loosening in my throat; the way I'd run from the shore for cover. *¡Donostia!* San Sebastián had awoken something inside me. I knew what Carmen meant about "her earth." For reasons I could not explain, this place had let me in. I was no longer a stranger here. I belonged. My heart swelled with joy. For the first time I could remember, I was happy, contented, *alive.*

Chapter 29

DINNER WOULD HAVE been better with Omar on my arm. Or Carmen to order the plates and plates of *mariscos* and *merluza* I watched being delivered to other tables. I ordered a glass of *rioja* as I sat at the bar, next to the open case of shellfish on ice; first a sidewalk bar window walk-up, now a bar and fish monger rolled into one. It occurred to me that Americans have much to learn from the Basques. I sipped my wine and marveled at the scene in the fish case below me. There were prickly orange creatures I later learned were called *txangurro* or sea spiders; massive lobster bodies; crab claws; glistening white squid; shrimp of all sizes; and small shell-y things with creatures inside that I don't have a name for. Men in three-piece suits and hats came in and stood around enjoying a glass of wine, while the women behind the counter wrapped up lobster in newspaper for them to take and cook at home.

The place was pure Basque and the menu was in *Euskera*, so I took the taxi driver's recommendation and repeated "*chipirones*" in Spanish while pointing to the squid on ice behind the bar till the waitress had understood me. It was the best squid I'd ever had: Pan grilled with butter, and the little purple heads, too, on a bed of caramelized onions. I finished the meal off with salted anchovies, a slice of Manchego cheese, and a half carafe of Basque wine called Txakoli. I left the bar tipsy from the bubbly white wine, eager to return to the little house on the sea that belonged to my father.

When I got there, I wandered from room to room, exploring the place like an anthropologist who had discovered a new city that told of the birth of civilization. I stopped at each painting, touched each book on every shelf; there were historical books, old maps, abandoned records, a black and white photograph of Carmen in a row boat. She looked radiant, her swim cap tucked around her ears, her shoulders broad and her arms strong. Another photo showed Regalado with a group of men who appeared to be *El Grupo,* photographed on the steps of a cathedral. The back was marked, "Cuenca, 1978." My mother might have been there then.

Upstairs were two austere bedrooms that had been cleaned out long ago. Just beds and lamps remained, but I placed my hands on each piece of furniture, each bedpost as though they were fragile artifacts from another world. I was looking for my father. *My blood, my root.* Between the books and unfinished prints, *He must be here,* I thought. When I had touched every corner of their home, I moved outside to the terrace with a blanket and the carafe of wine *Señora* Mariñelarena had left me. The storm had passed, but the sky was black, the sea even blacker. The waves were strong, and the mist sprayed from where it hit the rocks below. I stared at the sea, rocking myself gently, again hypnotized by its fierce rhythm.

The realization that my father was dead hit me suddenly.

There was no sound, no word, no telephone call, no bird's call. No ringing, no singing, no coughing—nothing. But the waves seemed to stop briefly as a sudden stillness enveloped me, as if the whole world had paused. Somewhere in me, I knew that my father had died.

I felt my body trembling. Beyond, the cold black sea of *Donostia* rolled and thundered on as it had done for a million years.

Chapter 30

I AWOKE ON the recliner in the sea-facing room of Regalado's home in San Sebastián. I knew with all certainty he was gone. I stretched, wandered to the kitchen, made myself a cup of coffee in the French press and was not surprised to hear Rafael's voice calling me from the steps of the little house.

Carmen sent him for me when news of Regalado's death reached her. He had died at 12:31 am. Rafael was in San Sebastián with a car eight hours later. He did not need to explain why he had come. I gathered my things and thanked *Señor* Mariñelarena who closed up the house behind us.

"How is Carmen?" I asked Rafael as we made our way out of San Sebastián and began the long drive back to Cuenca.

"Not as bad as I thought she would be. She is still in shock. But she is focused and calm right now, there is a lot to be done. His daughters wanted her to come to Madrid for the wake, but she has refused. You can go, of course, if you want to."

"What's the point now, Rafael? I'll just feel like an outsider there. There's no point—I came to meet him, to know him—what good will it do to see him like that?"

"I think Carmen feels the same way. It's too painful for her, anyway. He left her his ashes, so they will bring them when the funeral is done there in a few days. She wants to do some kind of ceremony with them, she wants you there…How are you holding up, Isabel?"

Rafael's question stung. I felt a sensation come over me that I would become hysterical, that I would start crying and would not be able to stop. I took a deep breath and it passed. Rafael watched me closely.

"*Bueno*, Isabel, if you are not ready to talk yet, I understand. Don't push yourself."

"No, it's okay—I am okay now. But you know, Rafael, I looked through the bookshelves and dishware last night, hoping to find some trace of him, of Regalado. I just wanted something, anything that I could run my fingers over, and feel his presence. But I didn't feel him, nothing. Not till I saw one of his paintings on the wall and I saw his signature at the bottom, in the right corner. It was this flowing black mark spelling out his name. And you know, it just killed me. That name will never belong to me—I'll never belong to it. It won't ever call me nicknames or tuck me in. That name, Rafael, never knew *my* name. And yet, these paintings, they get his name written on them, they get to be owned by someone. Rafael, I would have marked that name all over me, I would have written it on my arms, my knees, my toes, in permanent ink. And then, maybe I would feel like I belong to someone. Like maybe I have as much worth as one of his *cuadros*. It was the same thing I saw on the back of one of Carmen's records. *Regalado '76*.

"I would have done anything, Rafael, anything to have known him. I would have done anything, just to have sat for an afternoon with him, and talked. To hear him talk about his art, or about Cuenca, or *Donostia*, or anything at all. And now it's too late, I'll never know him. I just have these objects—these paintings, these records—that have a closer relationship to the man than I ever will."

My heart was racing and my breath had grown heavy. Rafael was listening quietly, afraid to move or say more for fear I'd fall to pieces. We didn't speak for several minutes, till Rafael spoke up.

"It's true Isabel that it's not fair, everything that happened. But at least you have his paintings. You can find him in his paintings. As a painter, you have his gift; you get to pick up where he left off."

Rafael put his arm around me and we drove in silence back to Cuenca's *Casco Antiguo.*

When we got there, I raced up the stairs to see Carmen. I suddenly found myself more worried about her than I was sad about my father's death. She came to the door like always, in her white apron, her silver hair fashioned in a tight bun. But her face was heavy and her cheeks were pale.

"Isabel, *pasa*."

Carmen took my hand, drawing me down the stairs into her home, and put her arms around me. All pretense was gone between us, and she just swept me into her, like the keys she kept in her apron. I felt the whole weight of what had happened begin to fall around me, and I began to cry heavy tears. Everything, the years of wondering who my father really was, the expectation of finding him in Spain, the grief that I had failed, that I had come too late, and that I'd never know him or be known by him. But I cried for Carmen's grief also; she had lived this story with him much longer than I had. As if Carmen could hear my thoughts, she suddenly lost her composure and began to cry. Both of us stood there, wrapped in each others' arms, sobbing.

"Why, why after all these years, after everything he did, is it so hard? Why do I love him still?"

"Oh Carmen. I am so sorry."

"*Ay cariño*, I know. It is unfair, so unfair...*pero, ¿sabes qué*? I promise you, if you will stay with me here for a few days, I will tell you everything. Every story is yours, the good and the bad, I will not keep it from you."

"But stories will not bring him back."

"No. But your father, he lives inside us now. And you of all people. You carry his gypsy blood, his depth, his immense creativity. His bulls, his love. You get everything but the *borracheras*, those I will keep for you, you don't need those… I see his face on you, recognize those eyes. You carry him in you and you don't even know it."

Carmen took my hand and led me to the kitchen where she prepared us bowls of green bean soup garnished with olive oil and crispy pork jowl. She sent Rafael with a plate to fetch some *jamón ibérico* from a bar downstairs. We sat in the kitchen and ate, and she began—true to her word—to tell me the stories I had waited my life to hear.

"*Cuando conocí a Regalado…*" Carmen began. "The first time I met Regalado was when my first husband brought him home for lunch one day."

"You were married before Regalado?"

"*Claro*," said Carmen seriously. "I'm a bit unique in Spain… and you know, Rego and I, we never married. It was illegal to get divorced while Franco was alive. So actually, I only finalized my papers with Juan recently. But that's a story for another time. Today, I am recounting to you how I met Regalado. Which is a sad story, but also beautiful:

"We owned a fishing gear shop in San Sebastián, Juan and I. We sold supplies and tackle to the fishermen. Regalado came to us one day, offering to draw our *carteles*—you know, posters to advertise the shop and whatnot. I was 29, I knew nothing of the world but what I'd known growing up in San Sebastián and a few trips to Paris to see movies and jazz men there. We had a beautiful life, too. We sold our goods during the week, and then on Saturday afternoon, we would put on our bathing costumes, pack a lunch of anchovies and Manchego cheese, and some fresh bread and we would go to the *bahía*. I would swim usually, and Juan, my husband, he would paddle next to me in a little row boat. We would cross the bay to the island of *Santa Klara* where we would take in the sun, eat lunch, and relax from the work week. Well, it was not so bad. And at the time I thought I was happy, fulfilled. What else did I know of the world? I was happy enough. Until I met Regalado.

"He was a tall man, broad-shouldered and towering above the other mostly short Spanish men. But he was thin too, you could tell he hadn't eaten well for many years. Few people did during the war, but the fisherman had always been able to provide for their families with their catch. They may not have had much money, but there would be *bacalao* and *salsa verde* on the table at lunch each day. Maybe not bread sometimes, maybe no meat, but salted cod, there was plenty. But you could tell Regalado hadn't had a woman to cook for him. He was married with two girls, but there was no love there—they were just trying to put food on the table for his two daughters. Juan brought him home and told me to put out a good spread.

"We sat together, the three of us, Juan, me and Regalado at our kitchen table, eating *bacalao* as we did most days in San Sebastián. Some fisherman or other would have traded us his catch for some line and netting. We ate, sopping up the *salsa verde* with our bread and Regalado told us story after story, with each tale we laughed harder and harder. I could not remember so much laughter filling our home till that day. So we agreed, Juan and I that Regalado should come back more often—he was hungry, you could see that, most of his meager salary he received from painting advertisements he spent for his girls to eat. We had plenty with the store, you know.

"So Rego came every Thursday for many weeks. Each time we sat for hours, past our *siesta* and into the evening, laughing, marveling at how he captured people in little gestures as he related something that had happened to him in his daily life. For a masculine looking man with shaggy brown hair, paint on his jeans and crooked teeth, he had no trouble impersonating a fat old *abuela* crossing the street or a flamenco dancer dancing *sevillanas*. He brought each of these characters into our kitchen every Thursday at lunch time.

"I looked forward more and more eagerly to each weekly visit. But without realizing it, over time, I also began to feel less and less well with Juan. With Rego, the world seemed so close, so beautiful, every person had a story, every moment became alive. Juan and I were great friends, and we are to this day, you know, I care for him very much, but he had never, not once in seven years, made me laugh.

"After six weeks, Regalado told Juan he could not come for lunch anymore on Thursdays. Juan, who had also grown fond of Regalado, could not understand why. He pressed Regalado until Rego told him. 'I'm in love with your wife, man. I cannot come back because I've fallen in love with your wife.' Juan told me that night in astonishment what Rego had said and that Regalado would be moving to Bilbao.

"When he told me, I agreed how crazy it sounded, how temperamental Regalado was. But an alarm sounded in me that did not stop ringing until I left Juan for Regalado one year later. I didn't tell Juan right away. Because I thought if Rego stopped visiting and if I went back to life with Juan as it had been, that the constant ringing that Regalado had set off would die down. Instead, it made its way into me, bored a little hole inside me and made me ill. I lost all strength and interest in my life. I went to recover at a farm outside the city, but nothing would help.

"Till one day Juan called Rego and told him he should come back and take me to Bilbao because I hadn't been the same since he'd left. It was then Juan did the kindest thing that anyone has ever done for me; he said if I loved Regalado that I should go be with him, because what kind of life is it to love someone you cannot be with?"

"So you left your husband?"

"*Pues sí,*" Carmen answered matter of factly, with a little glint in her eye.

"What did your family think?" Rebecca asked gently.

Carmen adjusted her position, then looked down at her hands folded in her lap.

'*Salvaje*' was the word my mother used to describe Regalado. She used it again to describe what I was doing to Juan. *Salvaje.* Savage. All of San Sebastián saw Rego as a wild drunk and a failed painter. They were not wrong, and I knew this as I boarded the train that would take me to Bilbao and into his arms. But I believed fiercely in him. In his capacity to love me as no man had ever loved me. I was bored with my nice life with Juan…Do not misunderstand me—my life with Juan was pleasant, sweet even at times. But it was only pleasant because I had had nothing to compare it to. The tenderness Regalado showed in boning a fish or peeling an apple was what most people brought to lovemaking. Juan was a good man. But Rego was magic.

"Four days later, I was on a train from San Sebastián to meet Regalado in Bilbao. I had cleared my closets for Juan so he would not have to look at my things, but I brought nothing with me except the clothes I wore. I could not bear to take money from Juan or the clothes or things he had bought me. He had tried to send me with more—the fine silk dresses, the jewelry he'd given me. Juan knew perfectly well I'd need the money living with Regalado, but I couldn't take it from him. I didn't want any of it. Even though it took me a year to accept it, when I finally admitted I loved Regalado, I committed right then and there to my fate. I said my goodbyes to Juan and to my mother who swore in my face as I left her. I boarded a train for Bilbao to meet Regalado. Looking back sometimes, it's strange that I made the choices I did. I had never surprised anyone in my life. I was the meek, reliable girl who'd swept my parents bar and stuffed peppers by my mother's side since I was old enough to walk. And me, Carmen, simple Carmen with not a cunning, daring bone in my body was leaving the only home I had ever known and the only man I had ever been with, and there I was riding a train to meet my lover who I well knew would never be a husband in the way Juan had been. And well, at that time, under Franco, I couldn't get a divorce from Juan if I had wanted to. Not for thirty years was I able to divorce Juan, despite living with Regalado that whole time. Every time I bought or sold anything of value, changed my bank account, for thirty years I'd have to write Juan and ask him to sign off on things. I was lucky Juan was such a good man; he could have made my life very difficult.

"But no, I couldn't go back to Juan after realizing I loved Rego. I had been Juan's little doll, his princess—he treated me so well. But Regalado, he did things to me without once touching me that Juan had not in seven years of marriage. I remember watching the scene outside the train windows that day as I left San Sebastián—there had been much rain and the fields were bright green, *verde, verde, ¿sabes?* Children stood by the tracks, waving their arms wildly at the passing train cars. We had done it too as children. I remember wondering if they knew that inside this train was a woman who had done every wrong a woman could do. If the passengers near me had known, they would, I was sure of it, have spit on me. But I was not nervous. No, I had committed myself to this new life. I had never expected it would be my life, but I knew, in a way I knew, it belonged to me. We had agreed to meet at the train station. Even though Juan had begged to drive me there, I could not be handed from one man to another as if I was an inanimate object to be passed among men. I had to make this journey alone. I had tried to imagine our first night together—with Rego. I tried to imagine what it would be like to make love to him and what we would talk about over dinner. I thought of the food I would prepare for him, how I would make our bed and bring him coffee and *cerveza* while he painted. When the train arrived in Bilbao, I got up calmly, in my white cotton slippers and simple skirt. It was smoky and crowded in the station and I wasn't entirely sure where he would be waiting for me. All this had happened so quickly, we'd hardly had time to plan for it. I looked around the train station for Rego—and then, there he was. So handsome, one of the few times he actually looked *guapo*, really *guapo*. He gathered me up in his arms, right there in the train station.

"I remember laughing in our bed, several nights after I had come to live with him. We were both not yet 30. I lay curled in bed. He had gotten up to work on a painting. I watched him, nude from head to toe, his legs and arms chiseled cuts of skin and bone, standing over the canvas. His hair was wild as always. And I can't explain it, but I felt that I was home.

"Those first months, before he met Zorita and was able to sell a few paintings, we lived in a room *con derecho a cocina*, that is what it was called—it was a boarding house, essentially with kitchen access. We shared it with 10 other people—it was a three-bedroom house. There was a couple and a baby in one room, Rego and me in another, and in the third bedroom slept four waiters during the day and four telephone repairmen at night. In the living room, by the door, on a mat on the floor slept the keeper of the house who made her living renting rooms in her home. Rego worked all day doing the odd publicity job he could find, and me, I cleaned houses. From time to time Rego's back would go out and he couldn't work, so we would live off my meager wages, sending half of it to feed his daughters. That was our life. Nothing about it should have been easy or simple. Making love should have been the last thing we wanted to do at the end of the day. But we did make love in that little room "with kitchen access," in silence, sometimes laughing, sometimes crying. I had never known emotion like I learned with Regalado.

Chapter 31

People came and went from Carmen's house. I got to meet the painters my mother had studied with. People like Gonzalo Torres, Andrés Padilla; Alejandro Soto and German Rojas had died a few years before but Soto's widow, Mercedes was there. They were old men and women by now, not the young revolutionaries of Rafael's stories and of the photos in the *Fundación*. People came from all over to extend their sympathies to Carmen. Even though my father had left years before, I learned no one had replaced Carmen's role in his life—despite the women who later floated in and out. It was as if Carmen herself was my father's home—not just the flat they had shared on *Calle* Alfonso VIII. Old friends and gallery owners brought Carmen flowers, flan, and homemade bottles of wine and honey. The flow of people was endless; Carmen had to post a woman at the entryway to let people in because she said she was too old to go up and down those stairs anymore a hundred times a day. She kept the dogs in her bedroom to keep them from running around like crazy from all the guests. I stayed close to Carmen, and she received people in the kitchen mostly. She met them like always, in her apron and Chinese white slippers. There was always a fresh *tortilla* on the counter, which seemed to materialize out of thin air.

Carmen did not put on appearances, even in the face of death. I listened to them come and go; I listened to their sympathies and their stories, and watched them smoke their cigarettes in Carmen's kitchen. They did not bother with me, which was well enough. No one knew I was his daughter, and for the first time since I had come to Cuenca looking for him, I was content to be an outsider. I wanted to absorb everything—in silence, without having to explain how I got here, or what it felt like to have come too late. Carmen seemed to understand this, too.

Despite the sadness that fell all around us, I was grateful in a way. At least I was here, at least I was privy to a world, *un mundo entero* as Carmen would say, in which my father had played a part. When the flow of visitors would slow, Carmen would tell the girl she'd posted at the front door to close up for a while to give us some space. Carmen would pour my mug full of warm milk and cognac—she said I needed some color in my cheeks and warmth in my belly. And then the stories would begin:

"Regalado was born in a little town outside of San Sebastián. His father was a fisherman, like most men there. He married a young woman—they called her *morena,* because her gypsy roots had made her skin dark and brown. Let me tell you, it was not popular then, or even now, to marry a gypsy. See, gypsies have roamed for hundreds of years from place to place across all of Europe. They performed theater and dance, sold things they had picked up along the way, and sometimes, they fought and stole. I won't say it's entirely untrue, but the Spaniards are not very kind to them in return. Some say if you have gypsy blood you are forever restless...and maybe Regalado was that way. I can't say for sure, but his mother's gypsy blood marked him a little. Anyway, that's where Regalado grew up, amidst the sailors, the fishing boats, the enormous black nets that came in each morning with their load of *bacalao* and *merluza*. Regalado grew up watching the fish with their slippery skin, flipping their way out of life like runaway hearts on the dock."

"How did the son of a fisherman become a painter?" I asked.

"Regalado loved the sea as his father had. '*Creo que soy mucho mejor pescador de truchas que pintor*,' he used to say. But it was not his sea in the way it was his father's. His father dreamed of Rego following in his footsteps, but Rego's heart wasn't in it. He kept up his father's dream until the day Regalado watched the fascists kill his father right on the beach. He was 13 and he watched them slaughter his father and brother, right there in front of him. Don't think it was uncommon either; I can tell you many similar stories of sons watching their fathers meet their deaths in the war and afterward during the *pos-guerra*. But Regalado, it affected him and he was never the same after. Not everyone is like that, you know? Some people get over life's tragedies more easily. Not Regalado. His mother decided to flee San Sebastián with her son until the war was over. She left their little house on the sea with a neighbor and tried to flee to France. But she was very sick and in the end, after they'd made their way through the Pyrenees, she had to give her son over to a French orphanage because she could not care for him. From there, Regalado became a little wild. He was passed between orphanages and ran away constantly. He was wild, it's true. But like most Basque men, man—could he cook. Basque men are the chefs in our land, and Regalado was no exception. It's true—they do all the important cooking. They have secret cooking societies that no woman can enter. One week someone will make *marmitako*, fish stew; the next someone will make squid in ink or a *paella*. And they teach each other like that. So that's how Regalado learned to cook.

"On Saturdays, Rego used to get up quietly before I would wake up. He'd walk the dog and then disappear into the kitchen. He'd use whatever I had in the house, he liked peppers and garlic, but he'd use whatever I had. If there was fish from Friday he'd make *bacalao* with green sauce. If we didn't have fish and meat, he'd make a simple tortilla. He'd cook, brew coffee, read the paper, all without an inch of clothing. Entirely naked! That's how he liked to be in the kitchen in the morning. He'd wait to hear me stirring and then he'd come in with coffee and fresh bread and talk with me for an hour before bringing me breakfast in bed. For years he did this. It was on Saturdays that I'd fall in love with him again. He was such a wild beast, but on Saturdays, how I loved him.

"By Sunday he'd be gone, but for this one morning each week, he was mine. We'd eat breakfast together, sometimes in bed, sometimes naked at the kitchen counter. And do you know, we'd laugh like we did when we first lived together in Bilbao. As if we were 28 years old and nothing else mattered. I used to ask him, 'How can you be such a brute all week, then win my heart all over again?' Regalado would nod, then he'd tell me again like he did when he'd been drinking, 'Yes I am an asshole. I don't know how you love me.'"

I could listen to Carmen for hours at a time—her words were like a soothing balm to the emptiness I felt after my father's death. She had the storyteller's gift too—she had a way of making Regalado, and all the other characters that had marked their lives, come to life.

Martes, miércoles, jueves—the hours felt like days, and each day felt like a universe. Rafael had not been wrong when he said I could live in these stories, and in my father's paintings. I was coming to see that, and it was healing me.

On Thursday night, Soto's widow Mercedes came for the second time that week. This time, it was just the three of us. Carmen told the girl at the door to send everyone else away—she wanted to spend some time with Mercedes; she and Soto had been among her and Rego's closest friends. Carmen sent for some *pata negra* and a fresh loaf of bread for a light dinner. We sat around her green-checked table with the windows open, letting in the warm summer air. It was a beautiful night and Carmen looked lovelier than I'd ever seen her—she shined that night. As we talked over wine and *jamón*, Carmen looked at Mercedes with a twinkle in her eye. I knew what she had up her sleeve.

"Mercedes, you see this girl here?"

"*Claro que sí*, how could I not see her? What a beauty she is, too!" She nudged me as she said it, "It's the truth, *guapa*."

"Do you recognize her, Mercedes?"

Mercedes put down her wine and ham and looked at me carefully. Then her voice got very low and quiet, "What are you saying, Carmen? What are you saying?" Mercedes repeated herself at least three times.

Mercedes sat there looking at me until all of a sudden, she caught on.

"*Coño*, she looks just like Rebecca," she said. "Holy shit, how can it be?" Mercedes asked Carmen, then looked to me for an explanation.

"Yes, it's me. I came to find Regalado."

"*Jodeeeer,*" repeated Mercedes, still staring at me.

Carmen turned to her old friend and said, "It was a shock. It took me a couple of days, I didn't know what to do with her—I passed her off on Rafael at first." Then Carmen looked at me, and seemed to be talking to me and not to Mercedes.

"But it's been so many years now. And you know, you know Mercedes how I loved that girl. How could I not welcome her daughter here? Even after what happened?"

"*Pero coñooo,* Carmen—" Mercedes said as she returned to the *pata negra*. "How you have done it all these years I will never know. You are the strongest woman on earth I think, the strongest woman, I tell you…And you, you Isabel, what balls you have. I salute you both. The strangest stories have come out of this house."

Mercedes looked at me and said, "Your mother… she—how do you say—*ha metido la pata*…she really messed up…but Alejandro liked her very much."

Then she raised her glass: "Well then, to Regalado and Carmen. But most of all, to you Carmen—"

"And to Isabel" Carmen raised her glass towards me and blew me a kiss. "How good that you are here. How good that you are here."

We sat in the kitchen till late. I was relieved that Carmen had shared our secret. I felt validated by it, as if all this was not some story I had made up in my head. That I really was Regalado's daughter, and could grieve among his friends without feeling like an imposter. I slept more deeply that night than I had since I'd arrived.

I did not wake till past ten, and was surprised that Carmen had not come for me. I hadn't heard the doorbell ring or the footsteps of visitors in the stairwell. I put on my slippers and threw on a robe Carmen had lent me and went to knock on her door. I heard voices from inside and it took several minutes of knocking till Carmen heard me. I heard her call up from the kitchen downstairs, "*¡Voy! ¡Voy!*"

The door flew open and I saw Carmen still in her robe and slippers. For the first time ever, I saw her with her silver hair down, hung around her shoulders. She looked like a different woman.

"Carmen, your hair..."

She smiled and said softly, "Come in, Isabel. There is someone in the kitchen I want you to see."

"Is everything okay? I didn't hear anyone come up the stairs today and I didn't hear you take out the dog either..."

"...*Sí, sí sí*, everything is wonderful. Come."

I followed Carmen down the stairs, the dog nipping at my feet, curious whom she wanted so eagerly for me to meet. As I turned the corner into the kitchen, I caught my breath.

There by the window was my mother.

She sat with a cup of coffee at Carmen's kitchen table as if she'd been there all week, as if she'd never left Spain at all and had made her home there for the past twenty years of her life. She looked tired, but soft, softer than I had ever seen her.

Chapter 32

Carmen had called my mother when she got news Regalado had died. She got the number from an old mutual friend of Zorita's. It was the first time they had spoken since my mother had left Cuenca, 20 years earlier.

I had not yet recovered from the shock of seeing my mother in Carmen's kitchen. The stillness between them was remarkable, with their newly-worn layer of forgiveness. It was as though in all the years they had been apart, they had never really parted, not unlike the way Carmen was still tied to my father—even after all the mess he'd created in her life.

Carmen left us to talk alone with a single demand: "I love you both a mountain full. Now, you and you," she said pointing at me, and then my mother, "Forgive each other."

I was bewildered. I turned to my mother once we were alone. With Carmen gone, I was speechless, my anger rising. Rebecca tried to break the silence first:

"—Izzy…"

"No Mom, what the fuck?"

"—Izzy I know you're mad—"

"Mad? You have no clue!"

"Izzy—if you will let me explain—"

"Explain?! Well it took you long enough! You lied to me my whole life, then when you finally did tell me the truth, you refused to actually tell me the full story. Then you show up here and I'm supposed to wipe the slate clean? Like nothing ever happened? What is *wrong* with you?"

"Izzy, I'm sorry."

I stared at my mother with rage. But for once, she didn't try and control my emotions—or hers. Tears welled up in her eyes and she extended her hand. I didn't want it but I sat down to listen.

"Izzy, listen…I have apologized to Carmen this morning. Nothing can take away what I did, but now I must apologize to you."

"Whatever—you don't have to—"

"—Yes, I do. I hid the truth from you for too many years, and it was not okay. You deserved to know who your father was without me lying to you. I was young, I didn't know what else to do. I thought it would be better to just forget everything. Then later, I thought I was protecting you. But actually, all of it was to keep me from having to face up to what I had done. I am sorry that you did not get to meet your father, Izzy."

I stared at my mother in awe and disbelief. Though she had never been entirely at home in her own skin, she seemed completely at ease now as she stood so casually in Carmen' kitchen. But I didn't know entirely how to handle myself in her presence—I didn't know how to relate to her like this.

"Izzy—*Isabel*," she smiled as she said it. "I know it will take more than an apology to you to settle what grew between us. I am going to work every day of my life to do better."

"I guess I don't understand why it was so hard to tell me the truth."

"Izzy, you can't imagine the shame I felt about what had happened. I didn't want anyone to know—not even my father ever found out the truth—I never told him about what happened in Spain. I felt like if anyone ever knew what had really happened, including you, that it would be too painful, that I couldn't handle it."

"But then I found out, and you still kept the truth from me, why?"

"I was stuck—I was still trying to bury it. I needed you to show me the way. Sometimes the simplest things are the most painful."

I looked at her, this unknown woman before me and thought how strange it was that we were here. That it had taken meeting in a Basque woman's kitchen in central Spain to bring us together. I knew my mother was right; it would take time for things to heal between us. But there she was, she had come, she had gotten on an airplane and *flown* here to make things better. She was in *Spain.* In *Carmen's kitchen.* And she was not angry anymore. I felt a flood of emotion run through me, my throat tightening into a thick ball as my chin quivered. But I held my tears at bay…I was still not ready to open up to my mother.

"Izzy…I always knew you were your father's daughter. You never drew nice happy dolls—you always drew bulls and birds, just like he did. You have the creativity I never did; I can write about art—but you, you can make art. You have his sensibility about life, his courage. Look how you came here, at 20 years old—you just stepped on a plane and got here."

"So did you when you were my age."

"Yes, but it was arranged for me. I had a place to come to; I was accompanied on a train to Cuenca by Zorita right into Carmen's arms. You came with nothing—you were risking a lot—you knew you could be turned away and you came anyway. I don't think I could have come under the same circumstances...What I wanted to tell you is..." My mother's eyes welled up and I saw how genuinely sorry she was.

"...Izzy, what I wanted to say, why I came here, is to tell you that I am...I am glad you were born. I am so eternally grateful that you belong to this universe, and that I have had the opportunity to watch you grow in it." Her voice broke, but she kept on. "You are so brave, so smart, and...you are an incredible painter. That fucking bull you painted! You nearly killed me!"

She smiled and then reached out to me, taking my face in her hands softly. "I'm sorry it took me so long to tell you. I am so very proud to be your mother."

It was the first time in my life she had told me she was proud of me. We stood in Carmen's kitchen, still unknown to each other, still unraveling the miles of distance we'd sown between us, as tears rolled down our cheeks. My mother wrapped her arms around me tightly.

"Izzy, there is one more thing I have not told you...I wrote to Regalado once after I left Spain. While I was pregnant with you. I told him I wished things had gone differently, I told him I wished I could take it back. To my surprise, he wrote back."

My mother took a worn handmade postcard from the table and placed it between my shaking hands. On the front was an ink drawing of a sailboat with a star for a mast. Twenty other unwieldy constellations spun in the background, painted by my father's hand. I turned over the card and read his uneven handwriting:

'Dear Rebecca,

The winter in Cuenca has brought a terrible frost.

Once again I have destroyed everyone I love most in life. Carmen misses you and I am sorry. I can never be her father. But if you keep her, will you call her Isabel? It was my father's mother's name.

Aside from these worthless canvases, it is all I have to give her.'

Con Cariño,
Regalado'

My name, of course, my name!

Not Izzy, but Ee-sah-belle. *Isabel.*

I wept in my mother's arms. They were tears of gratitude, not sadness. I remembered the words I had whispered to my father when I first arrived in Cuenca as I scaled its hills looking for him:

Will you admit me, will you say my name again, will you call me hija *and tell me how this story came to pass? My life is incomplete without you; my world is broken without this story, telling me where mine should begin.*

Before I ever went to search him out, she must have seen a glimmer of his drunken, half gypsy soul calling out through my eyes. My father, whose flesh was made of salt, oils, and the blood of bulls he'd knifed in his younger years, he called out to me before I ever knew his name.

In this way I know now, in the silence of his departure, and without ever having met him, I know that he wanted me and loved me. Of course he spilled out of me into dreams and doodles. He who came out of the Spanish Civil War with scars down all sides of him. He who witnessed his father—*my grandfather*—killed by a band of *fascistas* on the *Playa de la Concha*. He who carried all this in him. This and his mother's gypsy blood which they said had made him half crazy. The chaos he carried that he took to the women he loved. He tore into them with the violence that was his birthright; the same violence that had torn into him. His rage that tore apart Carmen's home before the night was over, the contents of their apartment thrown out the window in a pile on the street below. This was the man who birthed half of me. And his gypsy heart beats in me now.

I had learned his language in secret, studied his maps, his *cuadros*, and come like a refugee across an ocean to find him. I had found that *somewhere*—the hills of Cuenca, the sea of *Donostia*; I had found that *somebody*—that gypsy thief named Regalado—gave me my blood, my root, my name:

Isabel. Pintora. Española.

Chapter 33

Carmen clapped her hands and summoned us to her. It was after ten at night and I stood side by side around Carmen's kitchen table with Carmen, my mother, and Keiko, Carmen's Japanese artist friend. The window was open and a light breeze blew in from the *Júcar* river. Lights illuminated the enormous pink cliffs outside Carmen's window. Their beauty was a product of their dying, the erosion that would one day erase them.

Keiko stood akimbo in front of an enormous pile of walnut shells and palm leaves. She waited for Carmen to give the command.

"Keiko, where is the wine? Before we begin, we need wine."

Keiko went into the other room without a word, then returned with a bottle of red wine and another bag of supplies.

"Empty it here," directed Carmen as she pointed to the kitchen table. Keiko turned the bag upside down, emptying the contents onto the green-and white-checked table cover. Out came tree bark, corn husks, empty cans of bonito tuna, and string.

"*Primero, vino*," said Keiko in her accented, always-broken Spanish. Keiko uncorked the bottle and filled the glasses Carmen had set on the table. She raised her glass and offered a toast.

"To Regalado. For better or worse, we loved him."

"To Rego," chimed in Carmen. My mother and I raised our glasses in agreement.

Keiko pointed to the various materials and said forcefully:

"We make boats." Demonstrating with quick and effortless movements, Keiko took a walnut shell, cracked it open, removed the walnut and its casing, then commanded:

"In here, go the ashes."

Carmen left us, only to return moments later with a small metal box. A white sticky label on the top read, "Regalado Eneko." My father was in there.

"They brought it from Madrid earlier. Here." Carmen opened the box carefully, then used a teaspoon to pour a small amount of ashes into the walnut Keiko had just emptied.

"*Mira*, Isabel, take this spoon and you start." Carmen held my hand as we spooned the ashes into another walnut. My eyes began to well up.

"No, Isabel, *ya*, you can't do that right now, or we'll all start. When you feel like crying, take a drink of wine. Till then, just follow Keiko." Keiko served up a second walnut and I gingerly poured my father's ashes in as Carmen had done. The two women looked satisfied with their creation. Looking up at my mother and me, Keiko barked orders to continue filling walnuts.

We sat at Carmen's table drinking wine and filling walnuts for two hours. Carmen finished the bottle of wine first. She had every right. We worked till midnight till the ashes were gone and 100 walnuts sat neatly in a box on Carmen's table. The buzzer rang; Carmen wasted no time, people were waiting.

"*Ahora*, go get your jackets and some good walking shoes. Bring that flashlight from the cabinet in there, okay? Keiko, you help me take these…" My mother and I complied and Keiko and Carmen gathered the boxes of walnuts and palm leaves. We had no idea what Keiko and Carmen had in store for my father.

We met in the stairwell, looking like two pairs of thieves, heading out to rob graves at the local cemetery. In fact, it was just the opposite; we were returning him to the earth. We clomped down the stairs with our fingers still dusted with the ashes of my father. Outside, a group thirty strong met us with candles. Together, we made our way through the *Plaza Mayor*, then up the backside of the Old Town, then down the winding cement stairs that led to the bottom of the canyon. It was dark and I found myself laughing out loud at our escapade. A 74-year-old *vasca* in a white apron, a Japanese woman, and two Americans leading a group of Spaniards down to the river with pockets full of a dead man's ashes cased in walnuts. This would be the send-off for an anarchist gypsy painter.

We made our way down to the river in twenty minutes. I could see the river's calm, green-colored waters reflecting the crescent moon overhead. I loved this walk to the river: The pathways that zipped and wound down the hill by the tiny *Iglesia de la Concepción*, with its tree-lined courtyard, and the statue of Mary holding her son by the church's pink doors. Inside there was room enough for a man and woman to be married by a single priest. I would have stopped to sit for the rest of the night in the *Plaza de la Concepción*, but we were headed to the river and no one was waiting.

The river was likely freezing, a result of the altitude in Cuenca, where the waters flowed from cold mountain tops. Keiko pointed to the cluster of rocks she wanted us to walk towards. Without the slight moon and our candlelight, it would have been impossible to see. Carmen, graceful as ever, made her way to the riverside with the step of someone half her age.

The ceremony took place by the river, below the *Casas Colgadas.* No one spoke. But it did not feel strange or forced. There were children and older people there; Rafael had come, and Mercedes stood a few feet from Carmen; a man who I did not know came from Toledo and sang a psalm. He talked about my father, how they had met in Toledo at an exhibition. He described Regalado's passion for life, his ability to empassion others. Then he sang his psalm; it was haunting and humble, with words in some language I did not know that echoed across the river as we stood at the water's edge.

As he sang, at Keiko's command, we released the ash-filled walnuts on their palm leaf boats, accompanied by little candles to light the way. But they all stayed close to the shore, not wanting to leave us yet. Keiko placed the last pair in the water and gave the boats a gentle push. I watched the first boats begin to make their way down the river, one by one, some in groups. The candles lit the river as though constellations danced upon the surface. We watched each one, till they had floated around the bend. We stood there till there was no more light and he was all gone. Into the darkness, gone.

Carmen wanted to send Regalado off in a way that would honor him. A funeral at the church was out of the question. And Carmen didn't want to go to the memorial with his family in Madrid. So instead, she and Keiko had conceived of this plan to fill walnuts with his ashes and set the walnuts afloat. When we had finished by the river, we walked along the bank, leaving walnuts under tree roots, along pathways, at a bench he used to paint at; we made our way back to the Old Town and left a row of walnuts lit by candlelight outside his studio. Carmen was destroyed, but she wanted to do this for him, for the only man she'd ever loved.

We returned to Carmen's house, transformed. Carmen said she felt Regalado's presence.

"Do not cry," Keiko told her, "There will be time for tears!"

"Sit down. I need to speak of this grief," Carmen motioned to the three of us to sit at her kitchen table. We sat in silence and listened to her. My mother looked at me and squeezed my hand beneath the table. The past two days had been the most emotionally wrenching of our lives together, and also the most genuine. I wondered what our relationship would be like once we left Spain.

"Sometimes I feel like a fool that I loved him as much as I did," said Carmen through tears.

"I could have had another life altogether, but I lived this one. I had this clay inside me all along, before I ever met Regalado. But it had to be worked, had to be molded into something. And it was Rego who taught me how to mold that clay. He was so right about so many things. And I love him, I do love him, eh? And I think he loves me too. I'm sure of it. Even though we didn't talk about it, even before he died when he'd call me, we didn't talk about it. But I wonder, now that he is gone if I will go too. One day, years ago at one of Regalado's gallery openings in Madrid, after meeting Rego and I and seeing us together, a woman who they called a witch came up to us and told me that we would never separate. 'You will die together.'

"What does that mean now that he has died? Will I die? Will what is inside me close up now that he has gone? I can't, I cannot just forget about 30 years of life with Rego. Inside, not a day goes by that I'm not living with Rego. Now that he's gone, I think, I'm a little afraid of that, eh? A little bit, eh? In some way, I continue to live with Rego. And maybe that's what gives me the strength to be like this, to make decisions and everything. There is so much, there is so much that he has made me live through, eh? He taught me to see things, you know sometimes, when I'm going around and around about myself, I think, 'Christ, Carmen, all the other women your age are scared out of their wits, in their little easy chairs, they don't want to see a movie that might be awkward, they don't want to lose themselves in music, they don't want… They don't want to be moved; emotionally they're just parked in one place, like, like mushrooms.' But not me. I still love, I still desire…What power must there be in his goodness and his sensitivity, that after everything he did to me, that I could know beyond the shadow of a doubt that he is the best person I've ever known."

Chapter 34

DAWN CAME IN through the kitchen window and lit up the slanted ceilings of the little apartment till they looked as white as the bedsheets Carmen had hung to dry by moonlight. I awoke feeling lighter than I had since I had come to Cuenca. There was no more expectancy, no more anticipation about whether Regalado would welcome me or not. That part of the story had come to an end. I felt sadness, but also relief. My mother had slept in Carmen's extra bedroom, and we had agreed the three of us would meet for breakfast whenever we woke. I heard someone coming up the stairs, and knew for sure it was my mother, back from a morning walk. She knocked lightly at the door of the apartment, the same apartment, it occurred to me then, that my mother had occupied twenty years earlier.

"Izzy?"

I opened the door with a yawn, "Good morning!"

"It's a beautiful day out, just beautiful. I had a wonderful walk, over the Parador bridge, up around the mountain. She pointed out the window. There used to be an old monastery, before the Parador that's there now." I smiled at how much she loved her morning walks.

"What?" She asked me, suspiciously.

"You're just as though you never left. You belong here, Mom. It's incredible."

"I know, Izzy. I feel like I have come home. Can you tell?"

"Can I tell!? You look like you emerged out of the very hillside."

My mother laughed and I noticed that for the first time since I was a teenager, anger was no longer the first emotion I felt in her presence. Down the river with my father's ashes. What good would it do me now?

"Izzy. I had an idea this morning." I looked at my mother with no clue what to expect. I didn't know *this* woman. She looked at me with an air of mischief I had never seen before.

"Izzy, a long time ago, I promised Zorita I would tell the world about these painters. But I never did. I failed. And other than betraying Carmen, it's the thing I regret the most. So I was thinking...what if I mounted an exhibition in Los Angeles of their work. Would you join me in curating it?"

I looked at my mother and took a deep breath. Her apologies had soothed me a bit. I was still raw from years of discord and her dishonesty about my father. But this offer blew me away. I realized then it was our path forward.

"In a heartbeat, Mom."

She grinned like a wild woman and clapped her hands together in joy. Tears ran down her face and she put her hand to her heart.

"Isabel. *Que historias vamos a contar.*" What stories we will tell.

"Let's do it!" I said as I wrapped my arms around her and squeezed her like never before. We laughed and cried all at once. "Shall I come down for breakfast?"

"Yes," my mother answered as she wiped away the tears from her eyes, "Carmen was making a *bizcocho* as I was leaving. It should be ready by now."

I threw on a pair of jeans and a sweater and we descended the stairs arm in arm to Carmen's apartment. My mother knocked and then pulled out the key. Carmen yelled out from the kitchen:

"*¡Pasad!*"

"Carmen, I brought Izzy!"

"Come downstairs!"

We made our way through the living room, down the hall and down the stairs to the kitchen. Carmen stood at the bottom of the stairwell, beaming. Carmen was smiling so proudly, I thought she'd fall out of her apron.

"*¡Tú!* I have something for you, Isabel."

"For me?"

"Yes, for you."

We entered the kitchen and my mother and Carmen exchanged knowing glances. Whatever it was, they were both in on it.

"Sit down. Have some coffee."

I followed Carmen's orders and sat down at the green-checked tablecloth. There was a flat box, about two feet wide, but only an inch or two high. Beneath it was some kind of folder filled with an inch of papers.

"I have been waiting to give these to you. I wanted to wait until the time was right."

"What is it, Carmen? You're making me nervous."

"No, no, what are you saying, you don't need to be nervous. But before you open it, I want to explain about what you will find in the box." My mother stood by the window with her coffee; she smiled at me as I looked to her for an answer.

"*Tu padre*, he used to bring home the strangest things. Strange people too, mind you, but that's another story. One day he brought home a microscope, you know, to begin to study things more closely, it inspired him when he painted. But Alejandro, who knew about the microscope, he decided to start bringing Regalado dead bugs. You know, little *bichos*. So Rego started collecting these things, big spiders, moths, you name it. And he kept them in a box upstairs. I couldn't look at it, it was too terrible for me. But he began painting these bugs from this microscope, and this is what resulted. It was always one of his favorite collections, and mine too."

Carmen paused, then prodded me, "*Venga*, open it."

I untied the twine carefully from around the white cardboard box and lifted off the top of the box. Tissue paper covered what looked to be a book of some kind. I looked up at Carmen as if asking her if this was really for me. I wanted her reassurance before I went any further.

"Don't worry, it's yours now. Go ahead."

I reached into the tissue paper and pulled out the book. Thick black letters were printed by machine press onto the book cover. *Bugs* read the title. "Regalado Eneko" was printed along the bottom of the page. I opened the book and there, in messy scrawl, in the same messy scrawl I'd seen on Carmen's album covers and at the bottom of his canvases, was my name.

"*Para Isabel. Con cariño, tu padre.* To Isabel. With love, your father."

My fingers ran over the place where he'd signed the book to me.

Carmen said softly, "He had it sent from Madrid before he died. He didn't know you were here, but he asked that I get it to you." I couldn't remove my eyes from his writing.

"*Venga*, look inside, Isabel."

"Sorry, it's just that I can't believe he wrote this to me. I can't stop looking at it."

I turned the page and there on the most beautiful white paper, with perfect black ink was a drawing of a bee. Every detail had been drawn, then pressed by hand into a machine to create the lithograph. I had read with Rafael about the process he had used for similar books.

"This is one of his greatest works, Isabel. And it is for you."

I looked up at Carmen and my mother, both of them looking at me with the most love I'd ever felt from anyone. My mother came over and put her arm around me while we gazed at the *gráficos*, each one a world. There were bugs of all shapes and sizes, 17 images in all. Bees, mosquitoes, a fly, a beetle. He managed their subject with a grace and simplicity that was moving. When we had gotten to the last of the drawings, Carmen said,

"Isabel. There is one more thing."

"Carmen, how can there be more than this? This is everything I could have asked for, short of having met him."

"No, Isabel—the drawings, they are beautiful, but they are not enough. They are not nearly enough. You deserve so much more. But as it stands, we are flawed, us human beings, and Rego was no different. There is no point trying to find something for you among his things in Madrid. His daughters and cousins will have picked his things over by now. But there is one place they cannot own, because Regalado put it in my name, and I shall put it in yours. He gave it to me when we moved to Cuenca in return for my using my mother's inheritance to buy the studio here. He would have wanted you to have it, and I know with all certainty that it must belong to you."

Carmen set aside the box filled with my father's paintings and pushed the stack of papers in a brown folder at me.

"Here. The house in San Sebastián. It is yours now."

I stared at the folder Carmen had placed in front of me in disbelief. My mother and Carmen said nothing, but watched me carefully.

"Carmen, I can't...this isn't right—this belongs to you. You don't have to give this to me."

"I don't want it anymore—I don't feel like it's mine either. And besides, the request to give it to you came from Regalado himself. He said I could do what I wished with it, but that if you wanted it, he would like you to have it. What would an old lady like me with a dog in Cuenca do with that house up there on the sea? What better way for you to have a home in Spain? A real home."

Carmen looked at my mother and added,

"Rebecca, you know that this will always be home to you. Always—no matter what happened before, Cuenca, my home is home to you. But Isabel, your father was always a Basque, through and through, half gypsy, half Basque, and that is where you can go to find him. You can come here and you can find him, and you can go there and you will learn very much about who he was, and the blood that runs in you. And, then I know you'll return to Spain every so often and I will see you again."

I had no words for the generosity she had shown my mother and me.

"Carmen, how can I thank you? After everything that's happened?"

"What you don't understand, Isabel, is that I loved your mother like a daughter. And as much as I loved Regalado, I am ready to let go of him. You have just begun to find him. And it will be a long journey, a long time till you get to know him. But you will find him, like Rafael said, in his paintings, in the house in San Sebastián. It will never be enough. But these gifts are not about me, they are about you, and what is yours. They do not belong to me anymore."

I had been reborn.

That was his gift to me; that was Carmen's gift to me—at 20, a new life is born out of their pain. I don't need to have known him. His life, his dying, led me here to find him. I was born twice: To my mother, into her sadness, her betrayal, her grief at something she could not take back; to a father who would not know me. And at 20 I am born again, here in this room, in Carmen's kitchen where she'd waited so long for my mother and me to return. And here we are, this trio of women, our lives threaded with his, made and broken by him. And yet, he becomes less important now. He marked us. But our stories, our lives go on.

Carmen—beautiful Carmen. Her silver bun, her white apron starched and clean, she turns to my mother and starts to laugh.

"*¿Sabes qué?*"

"*¿Qué?*" returns my mother in perfect rhythm, in a Spanish I had never heard her speak.

"I should have thrown him out and kept you. "*¡Qué gilipollas!*" Carmen begins laughing even harder. What an ass. What an ass. *¡Qué gilipollas! ¡Qué gilipollas!*"

My mother and Carmen start to laugh so hard they can hardly stand. So hard they begin to cry. But they are not thick tears this time. Not the tears my mother cried as she left Carmen's house with me in her belly two decades ago. And not the tears Carmen cried when my mother left. Or the tears I cried when I knew I would never know my father.

These tears are thin, sweet more than salty. They are tears of relief, forgiveness and joy. For 20 years my mother waited to stand in Carmen's kitchen and stop hating herself for what had happened. For 20 years I longed for my mother to laugh and cry like this. For 20 years, we waited in silence around a story that felt so wretched before and now could be told through laughter in a kitchen overlooking a mountain, with olive oil *bizcocho* cooling on the marble counter.

Author's note

Regalado Eneko and María del Carmen Altamira León are fictional characters based on the real life couple, Bonifacio Alfonso and Maria del Carmen Flores (known simply by her friends as "Flores") who lived together in Bilbao and San Sebastián, and then Cuenca for nearly two decades. This story, while drawing upon elements of their lives, is a work of fiction. The memorial described to release Bonifacio's ashes down the river was based upon a ceremony held in Cuenca for the Japanese painter, Kozo Okano, by his wife, artist Keiko Mataki.

Bonifacio Alfonso died in Madrid in 2011. His work continues to sell widely and he painted until his death. Flores still lives with her rose geraniums in a casa colgada in Cuenca.

I am grateful to Flores for her friendship, and for telling her story over numerous lunches and late night dinners, over the course of many years. Thank you, Flores, for teaching me what it means to live, how to cook, and most of all, how to be a decent human being. This book is above all dedicated to you.

I also would like to thank my husband Ethan for his never-ending support throughout the journey of finishing this book; Thank you, Ethan for the constant encouragement to keep going, to get it done; and not least of all, for the creative direction when I'd get stuck. You are truly a light in the universe. To our daughter, Eden, in the words of Rebecca to Izzy: "I am so eternally grateful that you belong to this universe."

Many many thanks to Kate Jetmore for assistance with the historic and cultural details, for producing transcripts and translations from the recordings of my conversations with Flores, and also for helping me with final edits; thank you to Michael Gaylord and Laura Bergheim at Wordsmithie for editing assistance; Thank you to my mom and stepfather, Deena and Randy Stein for lending me the house in Joshua Tree where, with the silence of the desert, I could complete a full draft. Thank you to my father and stepmother, Tio and Janet Rogers and all my friends who never forgot how important this project was to me – who read my draft excerpts, and gave me the strength to keep at it. Thanks National Novel Writing Month which enabled me to pull a manuscript together that led to this book finally being complete after 15 years of turning it over in my head. And finally, thank you to Masha Beversdorf for producing the cover design.

-Con cariño, *Devora*

Made in the USA
Middletown, DE
15 May 2020

94631069R00126